C. 3

F
G   Gordon, J.
y
         The ghost on the
         hill

DATE DUE		
AUG 4 1977		
NOV 2 1 1977		
OCT 4 1978		
NOV 1 3 1978		
NOV 2 8 1978		
NOV 5 '80		
SEP 7 '87		
SEP 2 4 '87		
NOV 28 '90		

R I C

THE GHOST
ON THE HILL

JOHN GORDON

THE GHOST ON THE HILL

THE VIKING PRESS   NEW YORK

First American Edition
Copyright © John Gordon, 1976
All rights reserved
Published in 1977 by The Viking Press
625 Madison Avenue, New York, N.Y. 10022
Printed in U.S.A.
1   2   3   4   5   81   80   79   78   77
Library of Congress Cataloging in Publication Data
Gordon, John, 1925   The ghost on the hill.
Summary:When Grace returns with her son to live in
her old hometown, secrets of the past rise up to haunt her.
[1. Mystery and detective stories.   2. Ghost
stories]   I. Title.
PZ7.G6577Gh3   [Fic]   76–28316
ISBN 0–670–33784–6

FOR SALLY AND ROBERT

THE GHOST
ON THE HILL

ONE

'You're having second thoughts,' said Ralph, as he nudged the car up the steep slope of the little bridge and stopped in the centre.

'You can't stop here!'

The woman beside him licked her lips nervously, and he glanced sideways at her and smiled. There was no denying her good looks, the small, blunt-edged mouth, short nose and the clearly marked arch of her eyebrows over eyes that were wide now with an alarm that made her very young.

'You must make up your mind, Mother,' he said. 'Forward or back. Once over the bridge and we're committed.' He enjoyed straddling the stream, frightening her.

'The house is bought,' she said. 'You know we're committed.'

'But still you don't act as though we are.' He sat motionless behind the wheel. 'Once across the bridge, however, and that's it.'

'Don't, Ralph. Not here. People are watching.'

'That has never worried you.'

'Well, it does now.'

'These watchers,' he said, 'where are they?'

'There.' She dipped her head, partly to indicate where he should look and partly to hide her face.

'I see what you mean.' His tone changed, and as he spoke he let the car tilt forward and slide

7

down from the bridge. 'I think I shall like it here.'

They went down to a long, narrow triangle of green that pointed straight at the bridge. It lay between a row of cottages on one side and the stream on the other, and the far end was bounded by the churchyard wall. It was against this that two girls sat on a bench and pretended not to watch them as the car drifted closer.

'That's far enough, Ralph.'

She was giving him an instruction but he did not seem to hear.

'Ralph!'

At that, he eased the car half on to the grass and pulled up, but continued to stare straight ahead through the windscreen.

'I like the little one,' he said. 'The one with black hair.'

'Let's go up to the house, Ralph.'

He turned towards her. His looks were similar to hers except for the narrowness of his face and the tightness of the skin over his cheekbones that put deep vertical creases alongside his mouth as he smiled.

'We have all day,' he said.

'You haven't even seen it yet.'

'I haven't seen any part of your village. You've kept it a secret from me all my life.'

'I have done no such thing, Ralph, and you know it.' She was indignant, but it was useless for her to go on, for he had got out of the car.

He stretched and looked around himself, and what he saw made him forget the girls for a moment. He knew from the map that the village was at the head of the valley, but he had not expected anything as conclusive as this. The hills rose on every side, even by a turn in the road seeming to cut off the route by which they had entered, so that the cottages, the triangle of green and the stream were walled in by steep slopes and banked trees. The village, or all that he could see of it, was contained in a dimple of the hills.

'You didn't tell me it was like this.' He stooped to speak through the car door. 'It's like stepping into a room.'

'You like it?' She was keen now for his approval.

'You should never have left.'

He held out a hand and, permitting him to encourage her, she slid along the seat and got out.

The row of cottages was interrupted near the pointed end of the green by one that had been converted into a shop. 'Let's see what they've got,' he said, but paused, still facing the girls on the bench, 'unless you'd like to introduce me.'

'Don't be silly, Ralph. It's over eighteen years since I lived here. They're nowhere near that old.'

'We are both strangers, then.'

She bit her lip and nodded. The nervousness which had afflicted her on the bridge seemed to have returned. She wanted to get away from the public gaze, even if it was only two girls at some distance from them. She let him hold her hand.

'Father is responsible for this,' he said. 'Bringing you back against your will.'

'No. That's not true. We always said we would one day.'

'And now he's rich enough.'

'He saw the house advertised, Ralph. It was just right.'

'No doubt. A good buy.'

'That's not fair.'

He grinned. 'It's not the place nor the time, either,'

9

he said. 'This is your homecoming, Mother dear.' He leant forward quickly and kissed her.

'Stop it, Ralph.'

'Shy?' he said. 'I believe you really are a village girl.'

'Was. Once.'

A pair of white butterflies danced and slid in the sun before them as they began to cross the green and he had the absurd idea that the insects did not belong here, indoors. He paused to turn his head and again take in the cottages and trees, but the feeling of being within a room, a big communal hall, was intensified by the fact that the two girls were now talking to someone and the little group against the wall were very much as they would have been under a roof.

The third person was a small, plump woman who must have emerged from where the road ran around the corner of the churchyard and disappeared. He guessed there must be more cottages there because she wore an apron and slippers and obviously, judging from the purse she clutched in both hands against her stomach, she had just slipped out to get something from the shop. Her hair, going grey, was drawn into a bun at her neck, but as they watched she turned away from the girls and they saw her face. Ralph heard his mother draw in her breath, and he turned towards her, his eyebrows raised.

'It's Betty!' she said. 'After all these years.'

'You were bound to meet someone you knew.'

'But Betty! She was my friend.'

He watched the two women. They moved towards each other but hesitated and stopped ten paces apart. The little woman's plump face reddened. She was bashful and girlish, and her round, dark eyes took in his mother's clothes and then dipped shyly, aware of her own wrap-around apron and slippers.

It was up to his mother to shorten the distance between them and she moved quickly towards the little woman who looked up, beginning to smile.

'Betty!' his mother cried but, instead of a greeting, it seemed suddenly a different sort of signal. The smile vanished and the colour went as suddenly as it had come to the plump face. His mother continued to advance, sure that she would overcome whatever doubts were in the little woman's mind. But it was not the sudden appearance of a former friend, more elegant and more assured, which had brought the change. The woman was staring beyond her and beyond Ralph.

He turned. Almost in the centre of the row of cottages a door had opened, falling back into shadow but letting the sunlight glint on a brass doorstep. Between the glare and the shadow he almost missed seeing what was there, and then a very thin, brown hand came trembling forward and rested on the black iron rail beside the two steps down from the front door. An old woman emerged cautiously into the light.

Her skin was mottled and her hair was thin. She had over her shoulders a dark shawl that hung in two long points before her and reached almost to the hem of a black dress that swayed as stiff as a doll's gown just clear of her black shoes. She moved with the jerkily balanced motion of a toy out into the sunlight, and he saw that her face, as wrinkled and soft as a collapsed puffball, had its creases pulled into a species of smile. And she spoke.

'I seen you.' The old voice was so thin it seemed that the dancing butterflies would cut it off. 'I seen you, Gracie Jervis.'

Ralph glanced at his mother. She had backed away

and was close to her friend. They were holding hands like two children.

'I knew you was coming back, Gracie Jervis.' Her jaws moved without a sound as though, in order to say more, she had first to practise her words, and the women waited. 'Now I can tell my Tom.'

At the edge of Ralph's vision the woman began to move, edging away.

'I'll tell my Tom.' And already she herself was retreating, her black dress swaying back to let the doorstep glare. 'Gracie Jervis have come back.'

He watched her disappear and his mother's hand on his arm startled him, but he smiled, expecting to be introduced to her friend. The small, plump woman, however, was not there. Her grey bun was going away from them and the heels of her slippers slapped against her feet as she hurried.

'How very sudden,' he said.

'Let's get to the house, Ralph. Now.'

'Very well,' he said, 'Gracie Jervis.' It was her maiden name, and he had never before heard her addressed by it.

'Let's go, Ralph.' She was anxiously pressing on his arm, forcing him to go with her.

'What was all that about?' He nodded towards the cottage where the door was closing, jerkily.

'Nothing. She's just a stupid old woman.'

'Aren't you going to stay and meet her Tom?'

She released his arm and turned away from him, walking quickly towards the car.

'And you didn't introduce me to your best friend.' He caught up with her. 'What's going on?'

'Nothing, Ralph. I just want to get to that house.'

He got into the car beside her. 'At least they haven't forgotten you, have they, little Gracie Jervis?'

She did not answer and he noticed that she did not once look towards the cottages as he backed the car away from the green, and turned into the road.

The girls watched as the car negotiated the narrow point of the green and vanished behind the cottages.

'That must be them, Jenny,' said the larger girl, turning to her companion. 'That must be them new people.'

'Looks like it.' Jenny, splitting a paint bubble on the bench with her fingernail, did not look up.

'You don't fool me, Jen. You ain't that uninterested.'

'I don't like the look of them.'

The bigger girl laughed and folded her arms. She was not fat, but the seams of her dress were tight over the bulges near her armpits. 'Well, I tell you one thing, Jen. He have taken a fancy to you.'

Jenny pushed her long black hair back so that it lay behind her shoulders. 'She didn't even introduce him to Joe's mother.' She had a small, oval face on which her lips and eyes were so clearly and smoothly drawn that she looked much younger than she was. 'I think Joe's mother was offended.'

'That she weren't.'

'She was, Dot.' Jenny's long grey eyes clouded as she thought of the little woman scurrying home. 'Didn't you see how quickly she went away?'

'That weren't anything to do with it.' Dot's shorter hair bobbed around her face as though to emphasize her words. 'That were because they was frightened. Anyone could see that.'

But Jenny had not. She had seen the elegant, fair-haired newcomers come face to face with a small plump woman in slippers who, after a moment, had run away, full of shame.

'They was frightened,' said Dot indignantly. 'That old Mrs Goodchild frightened them. She'd frighten anybody.'

'She's harmless.' Jenny had hardly heard Dot's outburst.

'Harmless may be, but how would you like it if you had just come into the village and then was confronted by that old witch!' She pressed her folded arms against her stomach and pulled in her chin. 'And then hear her going on like that about her Tom. How would you like it?'

Jenny looked sideways at her, taking in Dot's angry face, but after a moment she turned away smiling.

'That ain't funny, Jenny Briggs.'

'Yes, it is, Dot.'

'No, it ain't.' Dot rounded on her, speaking in a rush. 'Tom Goodchild's dead. Tom Goodchild's been dead a hell of a long time and yet she still go to his grave and talk to him. You can't tell me that's a nice thing to be greeted with.'

'It wouldn't worry me.'

'Well, it damn well ought,' said Dot. 'And I'll tell you one thing more; that worry Joe's mother, and it worry that new woman, whatever her name is.'

'Grace Jervis.'

'Well, at least you heard that much. And that there Grace Jervis is worried; believe you me, she didn't like seeing that old woman again one little bit.'

TWO

Joe Judd watched his mother. She stood at the little window, looking out, her head half turned away from him so that he saw her outline against the white glare of the net curtain. It was a silhouette portrait, intensely old-fashioned, framed, and every detail delicately placed, even her eyelashes and a stray hair from the bun at the back of her head drawn against the plain background. And then she lifted one corner of the sheet she held and it made a white pinnacle in front of her and destroyed the picture. Joe, on the other side of the bed, reached for it.

'Sling it over,' he said.

'What?' She turned away from the window to see him leaning across the bed towards her. 'I was miles away.'

'I know you were. Sling it over.'

The sheet rippled across and for a moment lay in the air between them.

'She's out there again, Joe. Just standing there.'

They were both bending over, tucking the sheet under the mattress, and the whiteness was reflected in his mother's face, putting pale marks under her eyes and chin.

'I don't know why you let her worry you,' he said. 'Everybody knows she's mad.'

'She's like an old vulture, Joe, standing there waiting.'

15

He used his reach and strength to shift the entire mattress on its base. 'Waiting for what?'

She smoothed the disturbed sheet, not answering him. Sometimes, as though just to defeat his size, she was like this, involving him in some anxiety of her own and then refusing to explain it.

'Waiting for what?' he repeated, but she busied herself tidying the bed, apparently not hearing him. 'All right.' His broad, gentle face became firmer. 'Let's have a look at her.'

The room was small and he had to tread on the blankets heaped on the floor as he went round the foot of the bed. He stooped at the little window and put out his hand to draw back the net curtain.

'Don't, Joe.'

He looked down at his mother where she sat on the edge of the bed, small and plump and troubled, and he knew he should feel sympathy but a sudden spurt of anger at all women's fears obliterated everything else.

'It's only an old woman.' He pulled back the curtain. 'Look!'

The road outside was narrow, wedged between two rows of cottages, close to the green but hidden from it by a sharp bend. There was a gap in the cottages opposite in which a small wooden gate let into the churchyard behind them. The ancient, stooped figure stood there, dressed in black, one hand as yellow as a chicken's claw resting on the gate. Her jaws moved as though she was chewing and behind her there was a glimpse of gravestones on the slope.

'Mrs Goodchild.' Joe did not try to hide his revulsion. 'Just an old woman.'

His mother, hunched in her apron, was almost as shapeless as the mound of blankets on the floor. She sat silent as Joe turned away, letting the curtain fall.

'She's not even looking this way,' he said.

'I know that.'

'What are you worried about, then?' He heard the surge of anger in his own voice and knew it gave her another excuse not to reply. He stood where he was, stooping under the slope of the ceiling, and felt her misery drag at him.

'Mum,' he said.

She did not even raise her head. Her short, plump fingers drew a pattern on her knees.

'Mum!' He forced her to look up. 'What's worrying you?'

'Nothing. I'm just stupid.'

'I never said that.'

'And I've lived in the same place all my life and I've got no clothes to wear and I don't ever say anything intelligent. Look at me.'

He was, for a moment, bewildered, and then he remembered the strangers that morning and what Jenny had told him about the two women meeting. 'That friend of yours,' he said. 'That Grace Jervis they were all talking about. Is that who's making you feel like this?'

'What if it is? It's true.'

'No.'

'I say yes.' She stood up, still bitter, and when he went to touch her shoulder she shrugged him off.

He stood silent for a moment and then his thoughts went back to the old woman outside. 'And what has Mrs Goodchild got to do with this?'

'Nothing that I know of.' Her voice was quite cold, vindictively excluding him from sharing her thoughts.

'Because she knew you both? When you were girls?' he asked.

She shrugged again and turned to the bed.

'What's worrying you, then?'

His mother's back was towards him and still she did not answer. He had to get out. The blankets clung to his ankles but he thrust his way along the foot of the bed and pulled the door open. He thought he heard her draw her breath to say something, but he plunged down the narrow stairs and was gone.

THREE

'It has a slight smell of decay,' said Ralph.

'That's because it's been empty for a year.' His mother walked across the bare boards of the room he had chosen as his bedroom. 'It's bound to smell like it does.'

'I'm not complaining. I like it. It's the flavour of your village, the whole valley.'

'Not decay, surely.'

'No. Age. Everything is so old and still. Listen.'

They stood by the large window and looked out over the field of long grass that stretched from below them to the distant hedge. The big house stood by itself, set back from the road in a bare field that, like a colossal step, made a level space in the side of the hill above the village. Beyond the field, the hill raised a smooth hump against the sky, and below them the village was hidden in trees and gathering darkness.

'You can hear the place mouldering,' he said.

'Don't, Ralph.'

'Drifting away grain by grain to silt up the bottom of the valley.'

She turned away. 'Must you?'

He smiled. 'It's the melancholy of the evening, Mother.'

She looked down at the camp bed in the corner. 'Are you sure you'll be all right here?'

'Of course I will, Gracie Jervis.'

'Please, Ralph. It's years since I was that.'

'It suits you.'

'Not Gracie,' she said.

'Grace, then.'

'If you must.' She was silent for a moment and when she spoke again she did not look up. 'She didn't seem to know I was married. She didn't seem to think anything was changed.'

'The old woman on the green?' He guessed where her mind had wandered.

'Mrs Goodchild.' She murmured the name.

'You didn't seem to like her.'

'I thought she was dead, Ralph. I thought she must be dead long ago.'

'But she remembered you. Recognised you, Grace. You can't have changed all that much. It's a kind of compliment.'

'Maybe.'

She moved to the window and stood close to it but could see no reflection of herself. The glass seemed to have dissolved in the warm dusk, and for a moment she felt that the big square house hung like gossamer over the grass, keeping its shape only because the air did not move. She wondered if this vagueness was the sensation of coming home.

'I never expected to see her,' she said. 'I never expected to see Mrs Goodchild again.'

It was warm in the bottom of the valley and the light was dim. Jenny leant against the parapet of the bridge beside Joe and with him looked down into the stream that was visible only to accustomed eyes, although its sound as it folded itself over the pebbles reached them in small, tinkling bursts. On the other side of Joe, out of sight, Dot was talking.

'I don't see how they got here without us knowing,' she said. 'I mean all their furniture and that. When did that come?'

'They haven't got much.' It was Joe who answered, catching both of them by surprise.

'How come you know that?' asked Dot.

'I heard.'

Jenny pushed back a strand of hair, using the movement as a disguise to turn her head and look at him. The broad shoulders were hunched so that his head was thrust forward, sideways on to her, made more massive by the twilight and seeming too large for the delicacy of his profile. His small nose and the edges of his mouth were cut so finely they were almost feminine and made him, for all his size, vulnerable.

'Well?' said Dot. 'Ain't you going to say no more? Who told you about their furniture?'

'Mr Wilby.' It was Joe's employer, the only carpenter in the village, and the man he had left school to work for only a few months before. 'They asked him to go up there and get a few things done to the house.'

'Today?'

'No. Last week.'

'Last week!' Dot flung herself forward so that she could see around him and speak to Jenny. 'He have known about them coming for a whole week! Didn't he say nothing to you?'

'Why should he?' Jenny moved closer to Joe, but she knew that he was distant, sunk within himself, as he had been all day. 'Whoever they are doesn't matter to us.'

'Not much!' Dot retreated behind Joe. 'Only the first new people to come here in I don't know how

21

long, and neither of you two seems the slightest bit interested.'

'We aren't.' Jenny was stroking a cushion of moss close to where Joe, in his shirt-sleeves, rested his bare arm on the parapet. She let her fingers stray from the hair-like shoots of the moss to his arm. 'We don't care about them, do we, Joe?'

He shook his head but still he was far away. She drew back slightly, hardly knowing whether to pity him or be angry. It was Saturday and they should have been enjoying themselves, but he had descended into some private unhappiness.

'Well then.' Dot had a short way with Joe's moods. 'You ain't told us what they wanted Mr Wilby for.'

'A couple of things.' Joe's tone was level, uninterested, but suddenly relief flooded Jenny. He had very slightly shifted his head so that she alone could see his expression. He was teasing Dot.

'Bloody great ox!' Dot, provoked, punched his shoulder. 'Can't you make him tell anything, Jen?'

Jenny touched his arm again and, obeying Dot, spoke coaxingly to him. 'Why did Mr Wilby go up to the house, Joe?'

'A door was stuck.'

Jenny leant around him to speak to Dot. 'A door got stuck.'

'Thank you.'

'Anything else you'd like to know?' Jenny lingered where she was, her head so close to Joe that his breath touched her cheek.

'Yes,' said Dot. 'Ask him what Mr Wilby found out about them.'

Jenny turned her face up to him, letting her hair hang down over the parapet. 'What did Mr Wilby find out?'

'Not a lot,' said Joe.

'Not a lot,' Jenny repeated.

'Tell him he's bloody hopeless,' said Dot.

Jenny looked up at him. His mouth was as clearly marked as the carved lips of an Egyptian Pharaoh. 'Rameses,' she said, 'you're hopeless.'

The name was an old joke between them. 'Cleopatra,' he replied, 'I know I am.'

He leant towards her and their lips were almost touching when Dot's voice again broke in.

'What about her husband? Didn't Mr Wilby see him?'

'I don't know.' But Joe seemed to think he was being too brusque, and he added, 'They're well off.'

'Anybody know that!' Dot was scornful. 'They'd have to be to buy that house. What do he do?'

'Some sort of business,' said Joe. 'He's abroad now, I think.'

'Well, that's something.' Dot was silent for a moment, and then she tried a new line of questioning. 'Your mum knew her, Joe.'

Jenny saw the frown and felt his arm stiffen. 'Only when they were girls,' he said.

'What about her parents? Did your mum say who they was?'

'They died.'

Dot sighed. 'Well, I shall have to be satisfied with that, I suppose.'

It was Jenny's turn to interrupt and bring him back to her. 'Rameses,' she said.

'Not that.' He had straightened. 'Four-eyes.' And he lifted his hand to put the tip of his finger to the bridge of his wire-framed glasses.

'They suit you,' she said, but he had taken them off. 'They do.' She took them from him and reached up

23

to hook the wire over his ears. 'That's better, Rameses.'
It was true. 'Without them you don't look as though
you'd ever hurt anybody, big as you are.'

Dot sighed again. 'When you two have finished,'
she said.

Ralph saw the sadness in his mother's face.

'Are you glad to be back?' he said.

'I think so.'

'Only think so? You made up your mind over a
week ago, with Father.'

She nodded.

'He's rushed you off your feet again,' said Ralph.
'And now we've moved in and he's not even here.'

'I haven't even had a chance to meet anybody.'

'I thought that's why both of you came last week.'

'So did I,' she said, 'but all I had a chance to do was
get enough furniture in for us to live here.'

Ralph laughed. 'Poor you,' he said, 'and now
Father's dashed off again.'

'For weeks.'

'All the better. It gives us a chance to get this place
into shape.'

'I suppose so.' She sighed, still not free of melancholy, and Ralph went up to her and held both her
hands.

'And next time we meet somebody you know,' he
said, 'I'll make sure that you are not disturbed by
stupid old women from the past.'

He noticed that she held herself stiff to prevent a
shudder, but she lifted her head and smiled. 'Don't
worry,' she said. 'That's over and done with.'

'Good.' He took her arm and walked with her to the
door. 'A walk?' he said. 'Round the estate?'

'That would be nice.'

'You've hardly had a chance to see it.'

'True.' Her spirits were reviving. 'The day I spent here with your father was just one whirl.'

'So now we get to know it,' he said, 'and chase away the ghosts.'

Dot turned away from the others to gaze across the green. The grass was already hidden in a darkness that seemed to have seeped down from the hillsides, and lights burned yellow in some of the cottage windows.

She was bored. Joe and Jenny clung together, murmuring, and excluded her; not that she blamed them, because if Richard had been with her they also would have formed a tiny, private couple on the bridge. But he was away, playing for the cricket club, and she had had to stay at home to help with the children. She drew in her breath and let it go in a long sigh, resigned to this fact of life, but nevertheless bored.

A shadow moved across one of the lighted windows and vanished. She watched, idly waiting for whoever had thrown the shadow on the yellow linen blind to walk back across the room; but when it reappeared it was as a figure against another window further along the row. Somebody was moving along outside.

Dot was surprised, for nobody had crossed the bridge or moved on to the green from either end; she was sure of that. She strained her eyes, leaning forward over the parapet. The figure moved so slowly she thought at first it must be eavesdropping and she was pulling at Joe to make him turn her way before she realised who it was.

'Look.' She pointed.

'I can't see anything.'

It was true the figure had gone from the last of the lighted windows but she thought she saw it moving against the faint paleness of the cottage fronts, moving further from them.

'I thought she might be coming this way at first,' said Dot.

'Who?'

'Old Mrs Goodchild, of course.'

'Oh, not her again,' said Jenny. 'Not after all that business this morning.'

'Well, at least she might be able to tell me something about them new people. Better than some I know.'

Joe laughed. 'All right, Dot,' he said. 'Why don't you go and ask her?'

'Not me!'

Jenny stood with Joe's arm around her and rested her head against him. She relaxed so that his arm would tighten, taking her weight easily. 'I know what Dot means,' she said. 'I wouldn't go either.'

'And it ain't no good you laughing, Joe Judd,' said Dot. 'You wouldn't get nobody to go where she's going right now.'

'That's true.' Jenny rubbed her cheek against his shirt. 'I wouldn't even go with you.'

'And where's that?' said Joe.

'You know very well.' Luxuriously, Jenny let her head fall back so that her mouth was close to his neck. 'She's going to speak to her Tom.' She felt his chest heave as he snorted. 'It's true,' she said.

'Ask your mum,' said Dot. 'She know all about it.'

'How do you mean?' Joe's tone had changed, but Jenny knew she had power over him. She let her lips brush his neck, and left Dot to answer.

'We was there on the green when they was talking about it. Wasn't we, Jen?'

Jenny, nuzzling him, murmured, 'I can't remember.'

Grace stopped before the house was out of sight. 'I shan't go any further,' she said.

'Oh, come on,' said Ralph. 'We need to stretch our legs.'

They had circled the house and then walked along the overgrown drive out across the field until the track turned and dipped suddenly to run for a short distance between high hedges down to the road.

'Not as far as the village?' he asked, and when he saw that she hesitated he held out a hand to her and she took it. 'Your fingers are cold.'

'It's getting dark,' she said.

On their plateau the light was fading beneath the horizon, sinking into paleness behind the trees to let the darkness deepen overhead. Yet detail was clear, and behind her the house showed up sharply, but like a toy, every window pane and door panel and roof tile drawn hard-edged and plain. The whole house rested in his eye against her head, but smaller, as though she held it on her shoulder.

He smiled. 'You don't call this dark, do you?'

'It will be,' she said, 'down in the valley.'

Joe was staring intently across the green into the dark curtain of trees that hung in heavy folds above the churchyard wall and submerged it in shadow.

'That's terrible,' said Dot, 'to see her going there at this time of night. No wonder she make people frightened.'

'The gate's still closed,' said Joe. 'She's not going in.'

27

Dot said nothing, and he felt that he was being humoured.

'She's an old fool,' he said, letting his anger include Dot. 'She's mad.'

Jenny felt the warmth of his skin through his shirt and closed her eyes.' I think she's rather nice,' she said.

'Joe's mum don't think so.'

Suddenly Jenny found herself standing unsupported and almost staggering. His arm was withdrawn from her waist and he brought his other hand down hard on the parapet.

'Damned women!' His voice was loud, and the girls stood silent. He struck the parapet again. 'They see things! They invent things! They make things happen when there isn't anything there!'

Jenny, half afraid, said, 'What do you mean, Joe?'

'That!' He pointed to the graveyard. 'You all believe she talks to her dead son! You all believe it means something!'

'So it do.' Dot defied him.

Joe stood still, and there was a breathless pause as they waited for his onslaught to resume. The stream chuckled once beneath them and then smoothed itself as though to listen, but before he could say anything a branch seemed to sway in the depths of the trees against the wall and a different sound reached them; metal being drawn slowly over stone. It drew their eyes, and then they saw it was not a branch that moved but the wrought-iron plume on top of the tall gate into the churchyard. It swung inwards.

Dot put a hand to her mouth and whispered into her knuckles. 'That's terrible; ain't that terrible!'

And Joe lunged. Both his fists hit the parapet and then he thrust himself back and was moving quickly away.

'Where are you going?' cried Dot. He did not answer. 'What are you going to do?'

He stopped at some distance from them and turned, his outline faintly visible in the dusk. 'I'm going to listen to her.'

Dot reached for Jenny and clutched her wrist. 'Bring him back, Jen.'

Jenny eased herself free. 'You're not going without me,' she called, and walked towards him.

Dot, alone on the bridge, watched them come together but could not hear what they said and then, without once looking in her direction, they turned and went away from her.

Ralph said, 'I'll take you back to the house.'

'You don't have to.'

'And when I've done that and I know you're safe,' he said, making fun of her, but taking her arm, 'then I'll walk down to the village.'

She was smiling, shaking her head, on the verge of making him leave her there, when she glanced up at the sky and saw a bird moving on wide laborious wings towards the rookery on the far edge of the field. It would have to fly directly over the house and she knew it was because she was tired that she made it into some sort of omen, but she nodded, tightened her grip on his arm and went with him.

From the bottom of the valley the fading sky seemed to rest on the hilltops like the surface of a pond. Dot raised her eyes and saw a bird swimming like a black water-beetle high overhead. It was tiny but, the instant it disappeared, its raucous cry filled the valley with such a wide, echoing loneliness that she shuddered.

29

FOUR

Jenny went with him but he did not lead her across the green to where the gate had swung to and closed. Instead she went with him along the stream to where the road bent around the corner of the churchyard wall and narrowed between the rows of cottages where he lived. She thought he was taking her to his house to allow her to see him confront his mother and end her superstition once and for all, and she slowed as they neared his door. But Joe walked straight by it and she had to run two steps to catch up with him.

He had crossed the road to the gap in the cottages opposite and was beginning to open the little gate at the foot of the churchyard slope when she held him back.

'You don't have to, Joe. I know you're not afraid.'

'My mother.' He bent his head, looking at the ground, struggling to know within himself whether to say any more. 'My mother is terrified of that old hag.'

Jenny spoke softly. 'But why, Joe?'

'That's what I aim to find out.' He began again to open the gate.

'But you can't go in there. Not at this time of night. Wait until tomorrow.'

'That's too late. I want to hear what she says.' He put scorn into his voice. 'I want to hear what she says to her Tom.'

Still Jenny clung to him. 'But she'll see you.'

'Not where I'm going.'

And Jenny saw that it was useless to try to stop him. He pushed the gate and stepped through on to a gravel path.

'I'm coming with you,' she said.

He stopped then and, with the kind of serious tenderness that she loved in him, he held her shoulders gently in his large hands. 'Are you sure?' he said.

She nodded, and he stooped to kiss her. Her lips were cold, but she knew he would recognize that it was because she was afraid. He raised his head, and together they looked back across the road to his cottage.

'This is where she stands,' he said. 'Like an old vulture. Just watching.'

Jenny felt the muscles in his arms harden and very deliberately, but still gently, he separated himself from her and turned to gaze up the slope. It was very quiet. The headstones stood on the tilted ground like doors erected without houses, a strange city in which the dead moved, and she went into it with him, treading softly in the grass at the side of the path. It was airless and she found breathing difficult so that when he stopped near the church she found herself gasping. A path crossed theirs at right-angles and went away to the left towards the hedge where she knew Tom Goodchild's grave lay.

Joe paused, listening, but there was no sound. Not a blade of grass stirred against another.

'Where is she?' Jenny whispered.

He turned his head slowly. Away to one side, almost below them, the trees lay in a heavy roll of black shadow that hid the wall and the gate, and on the other side the hedge cut off the hills beyond. Behind them the church stood silent. The old woman could be anywhere, watching them.

'This way.' Joe took her hand and she crossed the path with him to step into the shadow of the church. But he did not stop there and watch, as she expected. Instead she found herself moving quickly along beside the church away from Tom Goodchild's grave to where the massive hedge closed in on the church and nudged the graveyard into a narrow corner.

'This isn't the way.' Jenny's voice was almost suffocated.

'It goes where we want to go.'

They had come to a little porch midway along the side of the church and here he turned along a grass path that led from it directly to an archway cut in the hedge.

'No,' said Jenny. 'That's the rectory. We can't go there.'

But then they were within the hedge and she held her breath against the smell of the dusty dark greenery until they were through and the rectory's blank windows faced them across a lawn. She was about to shrink back when Joe suddenly left her, turning sharply to follow the hedge downhill again, but now with it between him and the graveyard. She followed, not daring to go back, and within a few steps the rectory disappeared behind shrubs that grew along the edge of the lawn and made a thicket that pressed in close to the hedge.

'Joe!' Her voice was louder than she intended and he paused until she came up. 'Let's go back.'

He shook his head and for an instant she hated him, but she had to follow his broad back deeper into the shrubs until, at last, at the edge of the rectory garden, they came to a deep ditch. He slithered down the bank and stood in the long grass at the bottom.

'Jenny,' he whispered, and held out his hands to

her. What little light there was caught in the lenses of his glasses and blanked out his eyes. Faceless, he seemed to be reaching for her from below ground and she shrank from him.

'Jenny!'

His voice was urgent, almost pleading, and she let herself go down, sliding into the ditch and falling against him. Whatever happened was inevitable now.

'It's not far,' he said.

The ditch ran downhill along the foot of the hedge and together they followed it, his feet pressing down the grass to make a path for her and making the whole hillside whisper around them. She stumbled along behind him, not knowing how far they had gone or why he beckoned her to stop and then lay against the bank to look through the roots of the hedge. He called her and she climbed the bank alongside him.

'She's not there,' he said. 'Not yet.'

He breathed the words into her ear, but they were loud enough to untrigger a blackbird from above their heads and send it shrieking over the churchyard. Jenny started and clutched at the grass. The bird's shrieks subsided, swallowed in the silence, but Joe had heard something else.

'Listen!' he whispered.

The grassy hump of the nearest grave hid all but the tops of the gravestones further away. Another bird, also disturbed in the dusk, fidgeted among them, one wing thrust up, stupidly preening, but no sound reached her. Not at first. And then the faint scratch that a bird's claw might make on stone.

'Look.' Joe's mouth was close enough for his breath to stir the hair against her cheek.

In the space between two headstones a dark shape

33

was growing. The wing trembled near it a moment, longer and vanished. A deeper silence spread out from that point, swelling to wrap itself around them and as it did so she felt the muscles in Joe's arm stiffen.

He also was afraid.

The old woman stood there. Ten paces away. Facing them. She was as thin as a child and childlike in the way she stood, motionless, her eyes downcast and a sheaf of flowers held in the bend of her arm so that the long leaves rose to a point above her head. Like a bird's wing.

'Look at you!'

The old voice came scratching at them through the hedge. They were pinned to the bank.

'Just look at you!'

The twilight hung like a veil over the churchyard but they could see the thin hair drawn back to show the outline of her skull. After the effort of the words, wrinkles stitched her eyes and mouth closed so that no life seemed left within her. But she began to move on the soundless turf and her eyelids opened on a watery glare that seemed to dissolve the fringe of grass at the hedge foot so that she could see them hiding there. Jenny opened her mouth to cry out. But the eyes did not linger. The glare slid by to rest on something at the old woman's feet.

'You been restless.' She stooped to her son's grave. 'I got to freshen you up a bit.'

Jenny heard the old fingers busy somewhere out of sight, and suddenly she smelt the earth beneath the grass.

'There now, that's better.' The old woman comforted her son. 'Look what I brought. Ain't they pretty?' She held the flowers so that he could see them

34

where he lay, and Jenny heard herself whimper. And the old voice came again. 'You was right, Tom. She have come back. Gracie have come back. Both of 'em together again now, like they always was. Gracie and Betty.'

Ralph came down into the village through a long tunnel of trees. It was like going down into a rabbits' burrow, and it got warmer as he descended, and once again as he stepped onto the green he felt he had entered a room. But it was empty now, and dark. And then, on the bridge, a face glimmered and he walked towards it slowly as though he was a predatory creature in the warren and this was his prey. But Dot had seen him, and as he advanced she vanished so that when he reached the bridge the entire village was silent except for the stream chuckling beneath him.

The old voice was no more than a whisper, barely reaching to them through the hedge. 'You don't need fret any more, Tom. Betty know you're here, and now the other one have come back to you. She have come back to you, Tom. She have come back.'

FIVE

Joe looked at his father across the breakfast table. Mr Judd was, as usual, eating slowly, bending over his plate so that Joe could examine the delicate little bumps under the soft, pale skin of his bald head, and every so often he would raise his face as his jaws chewed deliberately and would fix his eyes vacantly on the middle distance. He was much older than Joe's mother; his fringe of hair and heavy moustache were quite white; and he was much shorter than his son, being only slightly more than his wife's height, but he was stocky and Joe had inherited the breadth of his shoulders as well as the mild blue eyes.

'Another hot day, Mother.' He spoke as his wife, fussing around them both, getting them fed before they left for work, poured his tea.

'It'll be like yesterday,' she said.

Outside the window the little crowded garden between the house and the stream was cold with dew. but the sun was coming over the hill like a lancer.

'Well, don't overwork yourself, woman.' He put his hand on her arm and made her sit down, speaking gently to her. 'You haven't got to tire yourself out, you know.'

'But I got things to do.'

'Just you sit there and have a cup of tea. Joe and me will clear away before we go.' He wore a waistcoat, unbuttoned, over his collarless shirt, and from a pocket he took out a silver watch. 'We've got plenty of time.'

Joe pushed back his chair. He could not sit with them. The old woman at her son's grave in the night was like a sickly dream that had lingered all weekend, and his mother was in it, caught up in the old woman's fevered mind, and she seemed to know it. She appeared at times to welcome it as a foretaste of doom. Nothing would make him tell her of the old woman talking at Tom Goodchild's graveside about her, but he feared giving himself away. He stood up, stacking the plates.

'No need for that yet, Joe,' said his father. 'You've got a minute.'

'Might as well,' he mumbled and went out into the scullery at the back and put the dishes in the sink. Through the tiny window he could see the road on the other side of the stream where the school bus was rolling sleepily into the village, its first call of the morning. Jenny, he knew, would be waiting for it near the bridge, but the trees and the bend in the stream hid it from him before it reached her.

Six months ago he had been catching the bus with her every morning, but now he wanted, urgently, to get to his work in the carpenter's shop. He hardly knew why, except that it was something definite. Everyone had expected him to continue at school for at least another year; he had been promising and there was talk of university, but he had ended it all suddenly and taken the job in the village when his mother became ill. Her illness had not lasted long, but for a week she had been in bed and for that time the words in all his books seemed to fade from the page and withhold their meaning from him. It was profound, deeper than anyone guessed, and to save himself he had had

37

to grasp something with his hands. In Mr Wilby's workshop the job was vacant and he took it.

His father, a farm worker alongside Jenny's father, had not approved nor had his mother, and at times he himself sweated with anxiety at what he had thrown away, but he had had no choice. The only real things were what he could make.

'I'll be on my way, then.' His father stood at the scullery door.

'I'll come with you.' Joe picked up the small khaki haversack that held his sandwiches and flask. It was not necessary for him to eat away from home, but he had done so when he was at school and he had come to enjoy unpacking his things on the bench he had worked at all morning, brushing a patch clear of sawdust and eating, dirty-handed, while he chatted with any of Mr Wilby's friends who happened to drop in. Often he would go with them to the pub for a beer.

He said goodbye to his mother and joined his father at the gate.

'She's looking much better these days, Joe.'

Joe nodded.

'It's having you at home, I reckon.' He smiled under his moustache and his small blue eyes, twinkling, glanced shyly up at Joe, acknowledging, as he sometimes did, that he also enjoyed having his son at work in the village.

'She worries too much.' Joe found himself speaking breathlessly, on the verge of telling his father everything.

'Women.' His father shook his head. 'They get like that.'

It was useless to say anything.

'But that friend of hers who's come back.' said Mr

38

Judd. 'They were always very close. Maybe that will take her mind off her troubles.'

They parted without saying any more, but all day the chill of Tom Goodchild's grave hung like a curtain between Joe and everything he did.

SIX

'No Jenny tonight?' Dot was by herself on the bridge as Joe approached.

He shook his head. 'It's Monday.'

'I'd forgotten. Her night for Granny.'

Once a week, Jenny walked a couple of miles down the valley to see her grandmother. Joe had gone with her and left her there, but he had been unable to settle when he got back home and had come out, looking for somebody to talk to.

'Will she be late coming back, Joe?'

'I don't know.' He leant on the parapet and began crumbling moss from the stone and dropping it into the stream.

'I just come out for a rest. Them kids!' Dot raised her eyes skywards at the thought of the house she had just left. 'My mum and me have just got the last of them off to bed. I tell you one thing, Joe, I ain't going to have so many.'

'What does Richard think of that? He's keen on kids.'

'Just so many and then no more. He'll have to lump it.'

'You're not going to deny him his rights are you?'

'Rights be buggered.' She punched his shoulder, laughing. 'And Jenny think the same as I do.'

'She's never said anything about it to me.'

'That's because you've never asked her. I don't

know what you two do find to talk about together.'

'Plenty,' he said.

'I'll bet.' She joined him dropping moss into the stream, but when she spoke again her voice had become serious, slightly accusing. 'You didn't ought to have taken her to Tom Goodchild's grave.'

'I know.'

'She have thought of nothing else ever since.'

'Oh, leave off, Dot. It was just a mad old woman. You're beginning to sound like everybody else.'

'Well, it upset her. You know it did.'

He let his head fall forward. His mother, Jenny, and now Dot. It was like a female conspiracy. He muttered savagely into the stream, 'Damn all women!'

'I heard that.' The voice came from behind them.

They both started at the sound and turned quickly, looking over their shoulders with their heads almost touching.

'Caught you,' said the girl who stood behind them. 'I wonder what Jenny would think of this. Or Richard.'

Dot's hackles rose. 'They wouldn't think anything about it. They haven't got minds like yours, Diana.'

'Oh there I go again,' said the girl. 'Causing trouble.'

She was tall and very slim, and wore a long dress in thin material that, although it was very full and hung loosely about her, nevertheless enhanced her slimness. She had a small, pale face in which her eyes had narrowed as she smiled but the deliberate elegance of the long, fine hair that hung below her slender shoulders was undisturbed as a white hand reached out gracefully to pat Joe's arm. 'You mustn't mind what I say.'

'We don't.' Dot's voice was sullen, and Diana ignored her.

'What brings you down here tonight, Diana?' asked Joe.

'Why, the thought of seeing you, darling.'

Diana's white hand sped back to its companion nestling beneath her chin, and Dot lurched suddenly against the parapet and leant over the stream. She longed to spit into the water.

'Where's Jenny?' said the little, innocent mouth in the pale face.

'She'll be back soon,' said Dot over her shoulder.

'Oh, what a pity.' Diana spoke directly to her, making big eyes in her direction. 'And I'd hoped to have this big man all to myself.'

It was a coy game she often played, testing people, and even though Dot was on her guard she was becoming angry.

'He ain't your type.'

'They're all my type, Dot dear. Aren't you, Joe?'

He grinned. No girl that he knew cared for Diana, but she was, in her way, attractive. The little mouth in the small face had a peaked upper lip that protruded slightly as though it was always on the point of sipping something, and the lips were moist. Dot saw his grin and her anger became a little spurt of fury.

'She ain't really after you, Joe. You ain't got her class.'

Diana looked at Joe, letting her elegant hands fall open so that her face was framed between them and she parted her lips so that her small mouth expressed an astonishment that was meant to mock Dot. Joe, caught between the girls, put a finger to the bridge of his glasses. Dot turned against the parapet, rested both elbows on it and faced Diana squarely.

'You ain't often down here of an evening, Diana,' she said.

'Not often.' There was a deliberate lack of interest in Diana's voice.

'It ain't worth your while as a rule.'

There was so much antagonism in Dot that Joe could not blame Diana for making no reply. He felt pity for her even though he knew she was acting a part as her eyes fell and her hands hung loosely linked in front of her.

'But it might be worth your while now, Diana.' Dot paused, then added with malice, 'Was you hoping to see the new feller? From the big house?' Her dislike made her go too far and after a long, defiant stare, she flung herself round to lean over the stream again.

Diana raised her eyes to Joe. They were full of tears and her tiny mouth quivered. He licked his lips and swallowed, but before he had a chance to speak she said, 'Goodnight, Joe,' and began to move off. 'Goodnight, Dot.'

She drifted down from the bridge and had almost reached the edge of the green before either of them spoke.

'Good riddance,' said Dot to the water beneath, but Joe was standing uncertainly in the centre of the road. 'Let her go,' said Dot.

'We can't,' he said. 'Not like that.'

'If you follow her that's just what she wants.'

'Don't be like that, Dot. She's offended.'

'Damned good job.' But Joe's words had hurt her and she was looking away, blinking, when he began to move off. Then she saw him and made a move as if to hold him back, but it was too late; Diana, disappearing along the road that went to climb the hill behind the cottages, was drawing him after her.

'Oh hell!' said Dot. 'What the devil have I done now?'

Jenny stepped out of the house just as the moon began to edge over the hill.

'That's a long way for a girl to go on her own,' said her grandmother.

'I'll be all right.'

'Why don't your young man fetch you?'

'I told him I'd be late.'

'Take care, then.'

'I will.'

'Goodnight, Jenny.'

'Goodnight, Gran.'

Her grandmother stood at the door until Jenny was out of sight and then went inside, still murmuring to herself. 'I don't care what she say, that's still too far for a young girl to go by herself.'

Dot watched them go away from her, willing Joe to come back, and her wishes seemed to be answered when Diana suddenly increased her pace and disappeared behind the cottages, leaving Joe on the green.

'Come on, Joe,' she said to herself. 'Turn back.'

As though he had heard her he hesitated, began to turn, hesitated again, and then made up his mind. He was almost running when the cottages also blocked him from view.

'You bloody fool!'

Dot's cry rang out uselessly across the green.

Jenny was still a mile from the village when she left the last knot of houses that hid in a cluster of trees filling a dip in the hillside, and now she was out on the flank of the hill. She smiled at the thought of her grandmother's fears. Joe would have met her if she had asked him.

'Diana!'

She was moving swiftly up the hillside through the tunnel of trees and chose not to hear him. Ahead of her there was a patch of greenish light where a single lamp at the wayside shone among the leaves. Joe waited until she reached it before he called her name again and this time, caught in the light and the sound of his voice, she paused and waited for him to catch up with her. He was slightly out of breath.

'You walk quickly,' he said.

The lamp hung in the trees outside a pub that stood alone, set back from the road and as blank-faced in the cold light as painted scenery. She was slow to turn towards him and slow to raise her head, almost as though she was performing before an audience and needed to emphasize her movements.

'You can go away,' she said.

'Why?'

'You don't want to have anything to do with me.'

'That's not true.'

'Dot thinks it is.'

He was about to speak when the door of the pub opened and somebody came out. Her audience was arriving.

'So you can go back to her.' Diana raised her voice and Joe, aware of the man in the doorway but afraid to look at him, suddenly grasped her arm.

'Let's get away from here.' He pulled her gently and for one tense moment he felt her resist him, ready to

45

make a scene, but then her thin, soft arm went limp and, almost meekly, she went with him.

Jenny's foot touched a stone and it jumped away from her like a little creature hopping in the roadway. The moon gave it a tiny shadow that ran with it until it trickled into the verge. When it had vanished she discovered that she had stood still to watch it, and her hands were clenched.

'Nobody wanted to offend you,' said Joe. Diana, her head bowed, made no reply. 'So will you come back? Down to the bridge?'
'No.'
He walked beside her because he could not free himself without seeming to be cruel, and they climbed higher, putting the whole of the village between themselves and Jenny further down the valley. Soon the road curved until it found a contour and levelled to run along the side of the hill and the trees thinned so that he saw the smooth dome frosted with moonlight. Then, at his side, Diana gave a small, throaty chuckle.
'You should not be walking here with me,' she said.
'I can do what I like.'
'You know what Dot would say.'
'Damn Dot.'
'You should be with your Jenny. Not walking up here with me.'
'Jenny need not worry.'
'No, Joe.'
She was taunting him, and he wanted to apologise for seeming to have harshly rejected her, but she spoke again before any words came to him.
'Dot thinks I chase after anything in trousers.'
'I haven't noticed it.'

46

'Haven't you?' Her eyebrows were arched and she was looking at him sideways.

'Not unless you came this way for a purpose, Diana.' He attempted to be flippant.

'What purpose, Joe?'

He pointed ahead. Where the road began to curve down to go behind the village a little spur ran straight on to disappear between high hedges. It was the entrance to the drive of the newcomers' house.

'You thought you might meet the new chap, I suppose,' he said.

Her little laugh trickled in his ear. 'That's what Dot said. And if Dot says so it must be true.'

Still laughing, she began to run.

Jenny walked stiffly past the place where the stone had vanished as though, in the moonlight, it had taken life and was lurking there, waiting to follow her.

She wanted to run and took one quick step, but lurched to a stop. Ahead of her a house loomed like a square-headed animal at the roadside.

'Where are you going?' Joe's call followed Diana into the entrance to the drive.

'Where do you think?' The words came back to him over her shoulder.

'Wait!'

'No!'

He ran after her but the drive was dark between the tall hedges and he paused. He heard the rustle of her dress.

'Diana.'

The gate had jammed open in the long grass and she stood just beyond it in the shadow of the ragged bushes.

'I thought I'd lost you,' he said.

'You never had me.'

She began to walk deeper into the driveway.

'You can't go in there.'

Once again her words came back to him. 'Why not? I'm supposed to be chasing him, aren't I?'

As Jenny came closer, a dog trotted from somewhere behind the house and stood at the gate. Its tongue lolled out and its teeth showed white in the moon.

'Good boy,' she said nervously. 'Good boy.'

The dog grinned.

Joe moved faster to keep her in sight.

'They'll see you,' he said.

'Who cares?'

The driveway ended suddenly, opening out into the wide field in which the house stood alone with no tree, shrub or flower bed near it. The moon shone full on gaping windows and smokeless chimneys.

'Nobody at home,' she said.

'You can't tell.'

'I'm going to look.'

There was a glint of light on the film of the dog's eye and on the wetness of his tongue, but he was silent apart from the panting of his breath as Jenny edged by.

Diana moved out into the open and Joe went with her.

'There was a lawn here once,' he said. The grass was up to their knees, even on the drive where recent cars had succeeded in making a double furrow.

'Like wading in water.' Diana lifted the hem of her dress to spin round and send out a circle of movement in the feather-headed grass. Suddenly she was running again, leaning into the moonlight as though it and not the air streamed her hair behind her shoulders. The grass surged silver around her and she let it rush, slippery and dry, through her fingers.

He watched until she was almost out of sight and then he began to follow.

Jenny came down down into the village where the houses hugged cushions of darkness to them and slept. It was very warm in the narrow road near Joe's cottage and she lingered in the gap opposite, but all the windows were lightless and she turned away to gaze almost sightlessly up the slope where the tilted gravestones clumsily raked the darkness.

Diana had vanished. The moon and the silver grass had, like an acid, dissolved her.

Sight came back to Jenny's eyes. There seemed to be a ripple among the gravestones; they moved like hairs on a pulsing skin. And then, behind her, a latch rattled.

'Joe?' Her voice was on the top of her breath as she twisted towards the sound. 'Is that you, Joe?'

His mother stood in the centre of the road.

'Mrs Judd!'

The little woman's plump face was rigid. She paid no heed to Jenny. Her eyes were fixed on something behind Jenny's back.

Caught between two forces, Jenny turned slowly.

High on the slope, where the path was a trough in the gravestones, a figure stood looking down at them.

Joe saw a flutter of movement behind the house and

49

ran towards it, making the grass thresh like foam around him.

'Diana!'

She stood in the moonlight as though in the heat of the sun, leaning against the wall between two windows, her head turned towards her shoulder and her eyes downcast.

On the slope the figure raised his arm to beckon. His arm came up, and as it did so it stretched towards Jenny. It reached out along the length of the path until the fingers were in her face and her eyes gazed into the blackness of a gaping sleeve.

She breathed black air. She was blind. And the fingers reached behind her and pressed suddenly and sharply in her back.

The roughness of the wall tore at Joe's bare arm as he thrust it behind Diana. Her tiny sipping mouth would not come towards him until he forced her to face him. For an instant the little beak pretended to be delicate, and then his lips unlocked it.

The sudden thrust in Jenny's back pushed her to one side. She staggered in the blackness and saw nothing, but there were footsteps, quick footsteps running, beyond her and away up the slope.

The little mouth was fierce and liquid, hungry for him.

Above Jenny a cry grated and echoed in the sky. There was a rook, poised in the light of the moon,

50

ragged-edged as though it had fifty heads all open and crying out.

Diana spoke meaningless words into his mouth.

Jenny whimpered. The rook rocked to rest in the black tree top. She was alone. The slope was empty and the road behind her was deserted.

SEVEN

Jenny knew that it was shock that forced this silence upon her. Great doors had clanged shut in the night leaving her alone in a corridor she must follow until she came out into the light, if there should be light.

It was the last day of term before the summer holiday, yet she sat alone on the bus coming home from school, gazing out of the window, not wanting to talk, and holding the events of the night untouched in her head. She had walked slowly home in the moonlight, gone to bed, slept and awakened with the same sense of stillness that surrounded her when she found herself alone outside Joe's house with the rook's cry still ringing around her. Now, beyond the window, she saw that the harsh sun put a coppery bleakness about the distant hills and made them into the dunes of a red desert.

Their emptiness was still with her when she got off the bus. And then, opposite Joe's workshop, a brown hen that had strayed from the farmyard across the road, fixed a hard, bright eye on her, blinked once, as if it was a magic sign, and brought her out of the long corridor into the light of the real day.

It had been Joe on the churchyard slope, Joe beckoning to his mother to show her that there was nothing to fear from the old woman, and it had been his mother, afraid nevertheless, who had blundered into Jenny so that it seemed to be his fingers pressing at her back.

Warmth suddenly came back to her and the stiffness in her muscles dissolved. She was eager to break her silence as she turned into the workshop yard. But Joe was not there. The workshop door was open and inside she could see and hear Mr Wilby at his bench. He always embarrassed her slightly, smiling at her as though he knew something discreditable about her, and normally she would hang back if she could not see Joe, but now she climbed the step and walked in.

Mr Wilby looked up. 'There's a sight for sore eyes,' he said and waited until she was blushing before he went on. 'That's just what that boy Joe needs to brighten him up, a pretty little old girl like you.'

'He doesn't need brightening up, does he?' She tried, in spite of her confusion, to face up to his teasing.

'Ah, well.' Mr Wilby lifted his cap slightly and with the same hand scratched his almost bald head. He was slow to answer, and Jenny found herself aware of the grains of sawdust on the bench and the fine powdered dust that filmed Mr Wilby's spectacles and accumulated in the folds of his apron. Joe worked in this dim, cluttered room, and liked it. 'I wonder you didn't see him just now, Jenny.'

'Isn't he here?'

'I just sent him home.'

'Is there anything wrong?'

'You have gone pale, gal,' he said. 'What a thing true love is.' Again there was his deliberate, agonizing pause. 'But you don't need to worry, there ain't a thing wrong with him that I know of.' He rested both hands on the bench, his thick, dusty fingers overlapping the carpenter's tools that lay there. 'He's worried about his mum.'

53

'What about her?' Jenny heard her voice and it was too loud.

'From what he say, she's just a bit down in the dumps.'

'Why?'

'No need to get het up, Jenny gal. It's nothing physical as far as I can make out.'

'Didn't he say anything?'

'You know Joe. He keeps things bottled up.'

She began to back out of the door, and Mr Wilby continued to smile at her.

'You go and put him to rights, Jenny.'

She nodded, going backwards down the steps.

'Lucky old Joe,' he said, 'I wouldn't mind being in his shoes.'

Joe left his mother and crossed the road. It was because they were so alike that she could make him suffer. As now. Her illness had passed but had left her weak, on some days worse than others, but it was not this alone which had plunged her into the kind of misery that had drawn him from his work. There was something else. Her silences had increased since her meeting with the newcomers, as though she brooded on some discontent or an anxiety from the past, and he was being dragged into the depths with her.

He opened the little gate and entered the churchyard. It was deserted now, full of the empty stillness he needed. There was nothing to threaten him, but the peacefulness did not bring ease. The sunlight was a glare of sickly lightning. He felt its heat but it chilled him and its brightness split the gravestones into a million fragments that were like sand in his eyes.

His mother complained of nothing, but her silences ate into him. She could not even suspect his betrayal of

Jenny, but she had sensed his guilt and remained silent, offering no comfort, as though she welcomed an unhappiness to match her own.

Joe walked through the grass and the scent of it rose and clung like the taste of metal in his mouth.

Her anxiety, whatever it was, worked within him. She seemed calm, she did her work in the house, but she was withdrawn, crouched within herself, curled up tight. She was waiting for something to happen. Once more, as in her illness, he was afraid for her.

He raised his head and looked along the slope. It was still and quiet under the sun, but his vision was broken so that nothing his eye rested on appeared complete, and his head ached.

She would not allow him to help. She let him watch her suffer and made him responsible for her misery.

He went into the shade of the church and rested his head against the stone.

Everything was jagged, torn apart – Jenny, Diana, his mother.

The cool stone gave him no relief.

In the tiny garden of Joe's house the bushes pushed close to the back door, and Jenny stood still, listening. She knocked, but the silence of the cottage was solid, throwing back the sound. Nobody was there; she was sure of it, but she waited until the handles of her bag, heavy with books, began to cut into her fingers, and then she turned away.

The door opened. 'Mrs Judd!' Jenny was startled.

'I was upstairs when you knocked.' The little woman's plump face was pale as though, inside the house, everything was cool.

'Are you all right?' The words came out quickly before Jenny had time to think.

'Of course I am.' The dark eyes in the round face were suspicious. 'Why?'

'Nothing.' Jenny shifted her bag from one hand to the other as though, by this means, she could cover the memory of the dazed face in the moonlight.

Mrs Judd's eyes held her for a moment, then her eyelids trembled and closed. 'I expect it's Joe you come for.'

There was a step down into the back room so that Jenny stood above his mother who now bowed her head, looking down to stroke her shapeless apron. She was so like a child who had grown to accept disappointment without complaining that Jenny suddenly wanted to put her arms around the plump shoulders.

'It doesn't matter about Joe,' said Jenny, 'I'll see him later.' She shifted the heavy bag of books again and they reminded her that the holiday had begun. 'And anyway,' she said, smiling at the thought, 'school's broken up and we've got all day tomorrow.' Every Wednesday, by a tradition of his own making, Mr Wilby shut the workshop.

'You have just missed him.' For the first time Mrs Judd seemed to speak directly to her. 'What a shame, Jenny.'

'Oh well.' Jenny shrugged but made no move to go.

'He was here just a little while back looking for something he needed at Wilby's.'

So that was his excuse to her for coming home in the afternoon. Whatever his worries were his mother was not to know. Jenny also lied. 'I thought I caught a glimpse of him.'

Mrs Judd hesitated, almost shy, and then she said, 'Will you come in for a minute, Jenny?' Some colour had returned to her face.

'All right. Just for a minute.'

'I know I ain't fit to receive visitors.' Now that her invitation had been accepted, she showed signs of alarm. 'Just look at me.' She glanced down at her apron and slippers.

'Well, we're a pair. I'm in my old school clothes.'

They smiled at each other and Mrs Judd stepped back to let her in.

'I've got the kettle on, Jenny.' She was confused, suddenly and unexpectedly happy to have someone to talk to. 'Or at least I will have if I can find it.' There was a colander on the table half full of shelled peas and the kettle was half hidden behind the sheet of newspaper she had placed to take the husks. 'Oh, there it is.' She bustled around the table. 'Put your bag down, Jenny. Anywhere will do. This place is such a mess.'

'I'll give you a hand.' Jenny moved towards the table.

'That you won't.' Mrs Judd tried to guide her to a chair. 'Sit you down and I'll tidy up a bit.'

But Jenny had already wrapped the husks and removed them and the colander to a stool that stood against the wall, and now she took the rest of the newspaper and began to fold it. 'I'm used to it,' she said. Her own house was little bigger than this and she had two younger brothers. 'I'm always having to clear up after everybody.' She patted the paper. 'There now, that's done.'

She held out the folded paper, but for a moment Mrs Judd did not attempt to take it. She stood motionless, looking at Jenny across the table.

'Oh, Jenny.' Her voice was very quiet.

'What is it, Mrs Judd?'

'I have been such a fool.' Jenny shook her head, but Mrs Judd continued, 'I have, Jenny. I have

57

been spreading misery all around me. Just like that poor old soul out there.'

'Who do you mean?' But Jenny knew.

'That old Mrs Goodchild; trying to involve other people in her own troubles.'

'I don't think she means any harm.'

'That's what Joe say. But she's always hanging around, making me gloomy. You don't know what it's been like.'

'I do.'

'Do you, Jenny?'

Jenny, with the little woman's eyes on her, nodded, and then risked hinting at what she knew. 'Old Mrs Goodchild,' she said, 'and her Tom.' It was proof that she understood and it made Mrs Judd pause. 'She frightens me as well,' said Jenny.

Mrs Judd sighed. 'I'm glad I ain't the only one.'

Now was the time to talk about what had happened, the violent thrust as Joe's mother had gone wild-eyed into the graveyard as the rook cried out, but the little woman was talking again.

'He were a nice lad, poor Tom Goodchild. A really nice lad, but everybody teased him.'

Jenny said, 'But not you.' She could not conceive of it.

'I didn't do nothing to stop it.'

'But you were only a girl; how could you have done anything about it?'

Mrs Judd did not seem to have heard her. 'All he wanted was affection, poor soul.' Shadows gathered in her eyes and her colour faded. 'I had ever such a horrible dream, Jenny.' Even her lips had suddenly gone pale. 'Tom Goodchild had come back and me and Gracie Jervis was going to meet him.'

Jenny watched. The brown eyes were unseeing, as

58

they had been in the night. 'Mrs Judd,' she said, but she was not heard.

'I was going to meet him, and Gracie Jervis was with me.'

'That was me,' Jenny said softly, but she was ignored.

'I saw him beckon and I had to go. He come for me.'

'No.' Jenny insisted on being heard. 'That was Joe, Mrs Judd. Joe beckoned you.'

'Joe?' She was puzzled, gradually coming out of her dream and becoming aware of where she was.

'Joe was telling you there was nothing to worry about. He showed you there was nothing to be afraid of.'

The blankness faded from his mother's eyes and a smile appeared, vanished, and came again. 'When I woke up this morning, I felt as if it had really happened.'

Jenny remained silent. Her words had not penetrated and his mother knew nothing of what had happened in the night. It was a dream to her, and Jenny was afraid to disturb it. It was enough that the anxiety had left the little woman's face.

Mrs Judd sighed. 'It must have been meeting Gracie Jervis that set me off.'

Suddenly Jenny was angry. 'She's got no right! She's got no right to make you feel like that! Why did she have to come back?'

'It's not her fault.' Mrs Judd's eyes were moist. 'We was always good friends, her and me.'

'I don't care. She's caused all this.'

Mrs Judd regarded her silently for a moment, and then said, 'Joe's just like you. He worry about me though I tell him there's no need. I believe he came back to see me this afternoon because I wasn't feeling too good.'

59

She put out a hand and Jenny held it. They were silent again, until Mrs Judd took a deep breath and said, 'I don't know how I come to be so lucky.' Her eyes fell, and then timidly, she raised them. 'You know what, Jenny? I'm going to tell you something now.'

Jenny waited. Mrs Judd's colour had returned and her eyes were bright with tears, but she smiled, the nightmare driven out.

'I know I'm stupid, Jenny, but I see you up the village the other day and suddenly the thought crossed my mind, that Joe of mine is a lucky boy; she's much too pretty for him. My own son, and I thought that!'

The strong little hand squeezed Jenny's fingers and then fell away and fumbled in the apron pocket for a handkerchief.

'If you start to cry,' said Jenny. 'I'll have to cry as well.'

Mrs Judd turned away, wiping her eyes. 'I'll put the kettle on.'

'And I'll get the cups.' Jenny knew where they were kept but it was the first time she had opened a cupboard in Joe's house. She was making herself at home and it was what his mother wanted.

EIGHT

Ralph brought in a tray and put it on the little table beside the low chair where his mother lay back with her eyes closed.

'It was a long drive, Grace.'

'But it's done.' She heard the cups rattle and half opened her eyes. 'Bless you, Ralph.' She lifted the teapot and began to pour. 'And you didn't mind being alone here all night?'

'Not I.'

She caught the enthusiasm in his voice and said, 'What happened?'

'Tell me how you got on,' he said.

'I wish your father had been there. You wouldn't believe the complications there are in buying an old place like this.'

'And we thought it was ours the instant we stepped inside it.'

'But it is now. Every last detail sorted out.' She closed her eyes. 'Those lawyers!'

'You should have let me come with you, Grace.'

'It was up to me to do it. You would have distracted me.'

'So you had doubts,' he said, 'right up to the last minute.'

She sipped her tea. 'Your father doesn't really know what it's like in a village. It was he who was insisting all the time.'

'Poor old father,' he said.

His tone made her glance at him sharply. 'Don't be like that, Ralph. He wants a place to settle.'

'And leaves you to do the nest-building.'

She laughed. 'Well, I signed. So that's settled.' She raised both hands, palms upwards, and looked at the ceiling. 'And this is your new home.'

'Thank you, Mother.' He bowed. 'It will suit me very well. There is never a dull moment here.'

'What do you mean?'

He smiled down at her. 'While you were away last night, Grace, there were happenings.'

She frowned, puzzled.

'Don't be alarmed, Grace. It was only lovers.'

'I don't understand you.'

'Outside.' He pointed. 'Lovers in the long grass.'

She closed her eyes and lay back. 'Really, Ralph. I thought it was something serious.'

'It looked serious to me. The moonlight glinted on his glasses with a white passion.'

'You saw who it was, then.'

'A big fellow. My age.'

'Wearing glasses.' She smiled to herself. 'I know him.'

'My mother would,' he said. 'All the young men.'

'I've never met him.'

'But you know him.'

'Wide shoulders?' she asked.

'Very.'

'Shirt sleeves rolled up?'

'That's him.'

'It's Betty's boy. Betty Judd.' She lifted one hand and waved it with an exaggerated limpness. 'Pour me some more tea, and I will tell you who the girl was.' She leant forward. 'But it must have been quite a disappointment for you to see that she already had a boy friend. Poor Ralph.'

'Well,' he shrugged, 'she seemed quite handsome, if that's what you mean. But not exactly my style.'

'You have changed your tune a little, Ralph. That little black-haired girl we saw when we first got here quite caught your eye.'

'Mother,' he said, but she was enjoying her revelation and he decided not to interrupt her.

'A sweet little face and big black eyes. Betty told me about her and her boy, when I saw her again in the village. Poor Ralph.'

He had been about to describe the girl he had seen with Betty Judd's boy, but now he changed his mind. They smiled at each other with mock sympathy from her and mock sadness from him.

He sighed, enjoying his deviousness, and said, 'Poor me. But don't worry about it, Mother dear, I still think I am going to like living here.'

NINE

The sun penetrated the single sheet that covered Jenny and woke her while the rest of the house was still silent. There was no school today, nor for seven long weeks of holiday ahead. As though she lay in water, she slid her legs and arms until she was spread-eagled under the sheet, and then she lay and listened to the chickens crooning at the bottom of the garden. The previous afternoon in Joe's house enveloped her, warmer than the sun. He had come home and found her there but he had said little and drifted away, returning to work almost unnoticed by his mother and herself because, absorbed in their new intimacy, they had not needed him. And he had stayed late in the workshop and she had not seen him again. But today it was different; she had much to tell him.

She slid voluptuously under the sheet and let the sun reach her again, and then she slept.

Her brothers thumped on her door as they went downstairs, and then she heard feet on the path outside and the latch of the privy rattled. Five more minutes. She put her arms outside the sheet and dozed again.

The bell was far away and she had been breathing slowly in time with the strokes before she became aware of it and then the sound of voices.

'Ellie.' It was Mrs Barker next door talking to her mother through the wooden partition that divided the two sculleries. 'Have you heard the bell?'

'Yes, Mrs Barker.' Her mother's voice was less shrill, but loud enough for Jenny to hear every word.

'That have been ringing for some time, Ellie. Is that tolling for someone?'

'It sounds like it.'

The voices had made sleep impossible and Jenny got out of bed and stood at the window. The houses, a pair of labourers' cottages, stood alone at the edge of the fields outside the village, and below her she could see the roofs of the two lean-to outhouses where the women were.

'Have you heard who it is, Ellie?'

'No, Mrs Barker.'

Jenny clicked her tongue in sympathy with her mother's patience. This far out of the village there was no way anybody could have known who it was, but Mrs Barker continued to speak.

'Listen.' The bell, hidden in trees far away, sent out a thin, uncertain note. 'One,' she counted. 'Two.'

There was a pause and the bell sounded again. Two slow strokes.

'That's a woman, Ellie. They're tolling for a woman.'

'Yes, Mrs Barker,' said Jenny's mother, humouring her.

'I know who that could be.' Mrs Barker began to list the possibilities. 'Her at the post office. She were a poor old thing last time I saw her.'

There was no reply, but this did not stop the catalogue. Normally Jenny would have listened, happily morbid, as the names and ailments and staying power of all the old women in the village were brought forward, but this was not the morning for it. She put on her dressing gown and went down.

'Here comes Lady Muck.' Her brother Ron, the youngest, was eating his breakfast.

She stood at the corner of the table and, ignoring him, called through to the scullery. 'Is there any water, Mum?'

Ron said, 'Plenty in the tap.'

'Hot water,' she said. 'Some of us wash before breakfast.'

'I do. I have to.'

'Do you, indeed?'

Her scorn was wasted on him. His eyes were on her, but he was already thinking of something else.

'Where's Will?' she said.

'Out the back.'

'Still?' She looked around the small, crowded room. 'This place is a pigsty.' Her father had been gone an hour but his plate and cup were still on the table where Ron had pushed them. 'Don't you ever tidy away?'

'What's the point?' He had her black hair and the same oval face and smooth, plump cheeks. His eyes were hers, too, and they stared at her vacantly. He was four years younger.

'I could kill you sometimes,' she said, and then she raised her voice again. 'Mum, is there any water?'

Her mother's voice came from the scullery. 'Use your eyes, can't you? The kettle's in there.'

It was on the corner of the table nearest the wall socket.

'You might have told me,' she said to her brother, but he chewed without replying and she pushed a chair into him as she went round the table to get to the kettle. It was full and hot. 'That's something, anyway,' she said.

'I want that.' He had come to life. 'I was going to make some tea.'

'Hard luck.' She went out and closed the door on him.

From her bedroom window she saw Will come out of the privy and walk towards the house. As soon as he was out of sight below she pulled her curtain wide.

The garden was long and narrow, cramped, like an extension of the little house. Neat rows of vegetables lay on either side of the path and at the far end, where a low hedge cut it off from the open fields, there was a chicken run with the grey and pitted earth half hidden by a honeysuckle in full bloom on the wire.

Jenny poured cold water from the jug near the wash bowl on the wide window ledge and then hot water from the kettle. The sun flashed on the surface and sent bursts of light wriggling into the dark corners of the room and over her skin as she stood naked in front of it.

The passing bell was tolling the years of the dead woman. Jenny lifted her head. She saw field after field under the sun stretching away to the horizon. The sound of the bell hung over the land until, lifting as it faded, it was absorbed into the blue sky. But at each stroke, in the instant before it vanished, it reached a fragile intensity that stroked her skin with the wriggling sunbursts, and she thought of Joe.

TEN

Joe sat in the back room and heard the tread of the women overhead. They spoke so softly their voices were no more than a murmur.

His father sat in the high-backed wooden armchair near the grate. His waistcoat was unbuttoned and he wore the clean white shirt, still collarless, that his wife had put out for him before they went to bed. Then, in the night, she died.

It happened again and again. Joe woke in the darkness with his father's hand on his shoulder.

'She's gone, Joe. Your mother's gone.'

In the silence of the deepest part of the night.

He had seen her once before the doctor came. Pale almost as the pillow, unawakened by the light on her face, by doors opening and closing, by voices or the footsteps of strangers in the house.

Dawn came, and the women, and he and his father washed at the sink. Joe stood on the cold stone floor and watched him shave and then bend over the wash basin to pass his wet hands over his bald head. Drops of water clung to the white fringe at the back of his neck and to the ragged edge of his moustache. He dried his face, and looked up, his eyes still wet from washing, and he seemed shy that Joe had seen him shirtless.

'All right, boy?' he said.

Joe had nodded and taken off his glasses to put them

on the shelf over the sink before he bent to fill the bowl and wash.

Now they sat and listened to the steps overhead. And then, even at this distance, Joe heard the creak and whisper as the bell turned over in the church tower before its black mouth bellowed. His father's hand clenched on his unlit pipe, and the bell swung up and yelled again. Two howls, then silence. A woman gone.

They were prepared for the sound when it came again, ready to hold it at a distance from them, but his father suddenly bent forward and shielded his eyes with his hand.

'The poor soul,' he said. 'The poor soul.'

Joe bowed his head towards the table until it rested in the crook of his elbow and let the tears flow from him.

ELEVEN

Jenny's hair floated and her dress drifted around her like a cloud, barely touching her skin, as she crossed the bridge. She knew how she looked and she began to run with the pleasure of it, but it was still early to call on Joe on his day off and she slowed as she came near the cottages.

His curtains were still closed and the silence was almost suffocating in the narrow road. She would end that for him.

'Isn't he up yet?' The back door was only half open when she spoke, and then she saw that the woman in the apron was not Mrs Judd.

Jenny blushed. 'Is Joe there?' she said.

'Come in.' The woman held the door wider and Jenny recognised one of Joe's neighbours.

She stepped inside. It was very quiet, as though the whole household was asleep. She turned to close the door; the latch clicked, and behind her the woman drew in her breath and let it out in a long sigh.

'Did nobody tell you, Jenny?'

The day lurched. Jenny kept her back to the voice and shook her head.

The woman sighed again.

Not Joe. Not Joe.

'Poor Mrs Judd passed away in the night.'

A grin she did not intend and then an avalanche in Jenny's heart.

'Sit down, dear.' The woman's hand touched her and Jenny clung to her arm as she turned. 'Are you all right?'

Jenny nodded.

'I thought you was going to faint.'

Jenny held tightly to the thick, soft arm and shook her head, but the room dimmed suddenly. She sank to a chair.

'Just you stay quiet for a minute, dear.' The woman held her hand and patted it.

'Where's Joe?' Jenny could barely hear the sound of her own voice, but the woman answered.

'He's with his father having breakfast up the road. It'll do them both good to get out for a while.'

Jenny looked up wildly. 'I saw her yesterday!'

'She told me.'

'Only yesterday.' Her tears were drawn down within herself, too deep to be released. Slowly, pushing down on the table, she got to her feet.

'You feeling a bit better now, dear?'

'Yes.'

Mrs Judd had not gone. She was still there; in the silence. It was her house. Her cups were in the cupboard, and the plates she had brought out only yesterday. She was still there. Jenny reached for the cupboard door but let her hand fall. 'I thought she was getting better,' she said.

The woman shook her head. 'She knew she could go at any time.'

Jenny again lifted her hand to the door but only to pull gently with her nails at its edge, not touching the handle. The door stayed closed. 'She died,' she whispered to herself. 'She's dead.'

'Yes, dear.'

Behind the door the cups were there, in the dark,

waiting to be used. Jenny could think of nothing but the cups hanging in a row, and then the woman spoke again.

'Would you like to see her?'

The room shrank and Jenny's muscles tightened and held her rigid.

'She was talking about you yesterday, Jenny. You and Joe. She thought the world of that boy.'

'I know.' To speak was to breathe again.

'And you. She was happy about you and Joe. I think she was happy when she went.'

The woman had decided what they would do. She moved away, bigger than Mrs Judd, already in charge of her neighbour's house and knowing that Jenny would follow.

The apron disappeared into the front room, but at the doorway Jenny paused, afraid. The light through the drawn curtains was dim and she was not sure what lay there, but the woman, moving quickly for her size, threaded her way through the crowded furniture to another door that stood at an angle across one corner. She opened it to show narrow stairs twisting sharply into the darkness and she began to climb, breathing heavily.

'These stairs!' Clumsily, she negotiated the bend. 'I don't know how they're going to get her down.'

Her bulk cut out what little light there was and in the blackness of the stair well Jenny swayed and had to clutch at the handrail against the wall.

'Ah.' At the top the woman let out her breath slowly.

On the tiny landing the only light came from a bedroom door that stood ajar. Jenny could see the foot of the bed, and the woman trod softly and whispered as though an invalid lay there sleeping.

'You don't need to worry. She's quite all right to look at.'

The bed was neat. Too neat for an invalid. The counterpane was folded back exactly half way and the sheet lay over the pillows. There was a shape but the neatness of the bed almost hid it.

Jenny stood still. It was not real. Mrs Judd was not there.

But the woman went around the foot of the bed, squeezing against the wall, and stood at the other side. Then, very carefully, as though what lay beneath was infinitely fragile, she lifted the white covering and stepped back with it.

The head was very small. No bigger than a child's. A mad child, pretending to be dead.

She will breathe.

Jenny waited for the sign. Waited. And listened. But the dead woman waited longer. Jenny's own breath shuddered and caught, like a sob.

'Isn't she lovely?' The woman put out a hand and with her fingertips stroked the edge of the grey hair on Mrs Judd's forehead.

The small movement locked Jenny's limbs.

'Don't she look peaceful? Just like she was as a girl. She were lovely in them days.'

The face on the pillow was pale, no longer able to warm the air around it.

'She were a lovely girl.' The woman's murmur crept into Jenny's ear. 'Really lovely.'

And Jenny said, 'She was.'

'You can see it, can't you?'

'Yes.'

It was there, the girl's face, appearing, ageing, and dying.

'She's like the rest of us,' said the woman, and Jenny nodded. 'It happen to us all.'

'Poor thing.' Very gently, the woman laid the sheet over the first dead face Jenny had ever seen.

'There.' The woman smoothed the sheet and looked across at her. 'You wasn't upset, was you?'

All fear had gone. Death happened.

'Nò,' Jenny shook her head, but downstairs, in the kitchen, she sank into a chair by the table and, hiding her face, she wept.

TWELVE

'Black suits you,' said Ralph.

His mother, lying back in the low chair, closed her eyes. 'Thank God it's over.'

'It was that gruesome?' he asked.

'I didn't have a hat. Everybody wore a hat. I didn't think hats were necessary any more. I should have known.'

'A veil,' said Ralph. 'It was a chance to wear a veil.'

'I may have a few wrinkles,' she said, 'but I'm not hiding anything. Not yet.'

'You have no need.'

His mother sighed. 'She was my age, you know, Ralph.'

'She looked much older.'

'Poor little Betty. What a life she must have led.' She opened her eyes and, rolling her head slowly from side to side on the back of the chair, looked around the large room. 'It looks very nice,' she said. It was the first room they had made habitable and, while she was at the funeral, he had been bringing in the last of the furniture. 'You have your father's taste.'

'A bit sparse.' He also looked around the room. 'But I like that. Space between objects.'

She let her eyes close again. 'It's peaceful here,' she said. 'And cool.'

He watched her. She was frowning slightly and he

could see her eyes move behind her closed eyelids. 'That little house,' she said. 'Afterwards they all crowded into that little house. I had to get out.'

'Did you not enjoy the funeral baked meats?'

'Ham,' she said. 'Ham sandwiches.'

'My poor mother.' He began to move towards the door. 'I'll let you rest.'

Outside, the heat shimmered over the grass and seemed to intensify the coolness and stillness inside the house. But suddenly a bird, flying to the rookery at the field's edge, cried out overhead, and she sat up, her eyes wide.

'What's that!'

'Only a rook.'

There was disbelief in her face, not at what he had said but at something else. 'It was horrible, Ralph!'

He waited, his hand on the door handle.

'When they threw the earth on the coffin.' She held herself rigid. 'It was like a signal. All the rooks in the churchyard suddenly poured out of the trees. Hundreds of them, Ralph. All making that horrible din.'

He opened his mouth to speak, but she shook her head, silencing him.

'And at that instant, directly across the gravestones where nobody else was looking, I saw that old woman.'

'Well?' Ralph raised his eyebrows.

'Mrs Goodchild,' she said, as though he had missed the point. 'She was staring straight at me.'

'She had a right to be there, I suppose.'

'But she was smiling! Right in the middle of Betty's funeral she was smiling at me.'

He leant against the door, folding his arms. 'And then?'

'Isn't that enough?' Her eyes were wide.

'Maybe it is.' He paused. 'For a superstitious village girl.' For a moment she did not understand him, and he assumed an accent. 'Was you afraid, then?' he said. 'Was little old Gracie Jervis frit?'

It was not until then that she saw he was laughing at her and she pulled off a shoe and held it as though she was going to throw it. He spread his hands in front of him, surrendering as he backed out, laughing.

The door closed and she let her shoe fall to the floor, her head sagging. 'He's right.' She spoke to herself, feeling the tiredness return. 'I'm being stupid.' And she had always liked the sound of rooks in summer. She listened again and heard them far away, like lazy machinery in a distant field. But the peacefulness they had always meant had gone and she crouched like a child in the chair and hugged herself because she shivered.

THIRTEEN

Joe stopped the van inside the entrance to the drive and sat there behind the wheel in the shade of the ragged hedge. He intended to go no further. A gatepost needed replacing, and Mr Wilby had sent him alone to the big house to do the work. Joe knew he had been given the job out of kindness, to help him survive the days after the funeral, but he did not want to meet the newcomers; particularly the woman. He remembered her perfume as she stepped inside the house when they returned from the church; it was wrong.

He leant across the seat alongside him to look out of the far corner of the windscreen. The house was out of sight, hidden by the curve of the drive, and the work he had to do was near at hand. He got out and slammed the door. From here, the edge of the plateau, he could see the whole valley opened up to sky, but the village was hidden below him, buried deep in the trees. He had been released from it and was glad to be here where the larks were singing.

Light-hearted for the first time in days, he opened the double doors at the back of the van where the new post lay. It was as pale as a coffin and a spade lay beside it. For one sickening instant the cold hand reached for him again, but suddenly he was in a fury, fighting it off. He hauled out the post and flung it to the ground, and then grabbed the spade and went to where the old post stood in the sun.

It was grey and rotten and shook in its socket, but he could not lift it cleanly. He hacked at the weeds at its base and began to dig, savagely, until the sweat trickled down his temples to the wire of his glasses. It itched and he paused to wipe it. His shirt was clinging to him and he took it off and dropped it on the grass and then, naked to the waist, attacked the ground again, undermining the post as though it contained all his unhappiness.

After a few minutes he threw the spade down and once more he braced himself against the post, one foot on either side, his arms around it, holding it close so that it rubbed against his chest and particles of lichen and moss stuck to his sweat. He heaved and it began to move. He shifted his grip, bent his knees and, with his face pressed against the grey wood, heaved again. It came this time, rocking with him as it lifted from the ground and he leant back holding its weight against the muscles of his belly, unwilling for a moment to let it fall.

The voice behind him said, 'You win.'

He twisted, lost his balance and let the post fall. It thudded to the ground between him and Ralph.

'Should I count it out?' The almost vertical creases in Ralph's cheeks deepened and Joe, seeing the calm amusement there, knew he was being tested.

'You can give me a hand to shift it,' he said.

'Gladly.'

Ralph was quite unperturbed and, as they stooped to lift it, Joe sought to soften the harshness of his greeting.

'I hope I've pulled up the right one,' he said.

'I expect so.'

'Don't you know?' Joe paused, crouched over the post, suddenly unsure that this stranger was the person he had assumed him to be.

'Why should I?' said Ralph.

'Wasn't it you who wanted it done?'

'My mother,' said Ralph. 'She's been taking all the decisions.'

So Joe was not mistaken, but once again Ralph had subtly taken the upper hand, and now he said, 'Where do you want it shifted?'

'Beside the van.'

'Together then. Lift.'

'Wait.' Joe cancelled Ralph's order. He would not accept him as an employer. 'I want it turned round the other way.'

'As you wish.'

Once again Ralph's acceptance was mild, making Joe appear harsh.

'All right.' He spoke more gently as they bent to the post. 'Up.'

They lifted, turning in the drive until Joe was backing towards the van.

'Bloody heavy,' said Ralph.

'Bloody is,' said Joe.

Their eyes met. Each stern face found it impossible not to smirk, but each fought to prevent it. Ralph, biting his lip, twisted his head back and caught sight of something in the sky.

'There's a lark up there,' he said.

'A what?'

Ralph put on an accent, a townsman's idea of a countryman. 'A bloody little old lark, hoigh in the skoi.'

Joe outdid him. 'Hark at the little bugger go,' he said.

They looked at each other along the post and their laughter burst out. They began to stagger but refused to drop the post and as they dipped and swerved they laughed more until, at last, they sank with it and crouched on all fours, facing each other, wheezing and red-faced and helpless.

'What's amusing you two?'

The woman's voice was above and behind Joe's naked back. He left it to Ralph to look up and reply.

'It's Joe Judd.'

'I know who it is,' she said.

'I found him . . .' Ralph gulped '. . . in intimate embrace with this thing.' He patted the post and as he collapsed over it again he just managed to say through his laughter, 'Just as though it was a girl . . . in the long grass.'

Joe stood up, wiping the grime from his chest and belly. His own laughter had faded.

'Pay no attention to him,' she said, nodding towards Ralph.

'No,' he said.

'Look at him; giggling like a child.' Now that they were out in the open, no longer in the little house where they had met, she was not as tall as he remembered. She smiled down at the collapsed figure of her son and then turned towards Joe, characteristically putting a hand through her thick fair hair as she said, 'I do like someone who can act his age.' The blue eyes regarded him, testing him as her son had done but swiftly coming to a conclusion. 'We must make allowances for him, Joe,' she said.

Ralph got to his feet, still gasping.

'Beware of him, Grace, he's a lady killer. Never trust him in the long grass.'

Ralph began to laugh again and she looked at Joe, raising her eyebrows. 'I don't know what he's talking about.'

'Nor me,' said Joe.

'Whatever it is,' she said, 'you can expect it to be nonsense.'

Joe nodded and she smiled that he should agree with her. 'What I really came down here for,' she said, 'was to tell you there's some coffee if you want it.'

She turned, as swiftly as a girl, and left them.

'That's Grace,' said Ralph. 'Take it or leave it.'

Joe picked up his shirt and together he and Ralph began to follow her. There was a trace of her perfume in the narrow lane but he knew it was stupid to let it remind him of the funeral. It was more the scent of summer, and as he walked listening to Ralph he noticed, as though it had just happened, that the sun was shining.

FOURTEEN

His mother's death was a barrier between them, unbelievably large. Jenny had spoken to Joe only once since it happened and then there had been other people present and he had been pale and almost silent. She had expected to bring him sympathy, even to weep with him when she told him how close she and his mother had been just before she died, but whenever she had called at the cottage he had been out, spirited away by a neighbour or a relative, and it was not until the funeral that she had seen him again. And then he was at his father's side, enduring the agony of it with him, and she had not gone near.

Then there came a day when she knew he must be back at work and she had found excuses to linger near the workshop but she had not seen him, nor that night, nor the next day until, late in the afternoon, she took her mother's bag and went shopping in the village. She delayed returning home until it was almost the time she would, during term, have got off the school bus, and then she went to the workshop. Mr Wilby saw her and sent Joe to her.

He came out into the sun, still pale, and they were both nervous, barely smiling at each other.

'I called for you last night,' she said. 'There was nobody at home.'

'Dad was there.'

'No.' She shook her head. 'Nobody.'

83

'He must have gone along the road,' said Joe.
'They've been giving him his meals there.'

'What about you?'

'Me too. When I feel like it.'

He may have been there, but he was not saying.
There was a silence. She could not ask him outright.

After a moment he reached for the bag she carried.
'Let me take that,' he said.

'No, it's all right. It's not heavy.' She drew slightly
away from him, and he made no further effort to help
her but he walked with her out of the yard and along
the lane as he did when she came home from school.

He squinted up at the sun. 'It's hot,' he said, and
it was like a stranger making conversation.

He was not going to tell her anything and Jenny
bit her lip, afraid to answer in case her voice should
tremble.

'Every day's the same,' he repeated. 'Hot.'

'Where were you, Joe?' The words came suddenly,
in spite of what she had decided, but she did not look
at him.

'When?'

'Last night.'

He paused for no longer than a fraction of a second
but it was enough. A needle probed for and touched a
deep nerve.

'I was working up at the big house,' he said.

'Oh.' Still she gazed ahead.

'It took longer than I thought.'

'Yes.'

They both knew he was lying. He would not have
been at work that late. He had gone back in the evening because they had invited him, and he had not
thought of Jenny.

'Are they nice?' she asked.

'I like them.'

'She's very pretty.'

'Who?'

'His mother, of course. I saw her the day they arrived.'

'Did you?' He seemed barely interested and there was again silence between them as they walked to the bend where, normally, he would leave her. They stood awkwardly until Jenny, shaking her hair back over shoulders, made one last try to bridge the gap between them.

'Diana would be envious,' she said.

'Diana?' He spoke sharply. 'Why Diana?'

'She's been hanging about, that's all, while you've been away.'

He had forgotten Diana. Like everything else, she was in some distant past. Only once, as he went towards the big house with Ralph, had he thought of Diana and the moonlight on the long grass and it had seemed an incident easy to forget. The newcomers had obliterated her from his mind; the mother who seemed only slightly older than her son, and both of them relaxed and easy, healing his wounds by not mentioning them. Now Jenny was forcing Diana at him again.

'Diana!' He let scorn thicken his voice.

'You know what she's like, Joe. She'll want to get in with them if she can.'

He said nothing and she watched his face, but he kept his profile towards her, hiding whatever secrets he had.

'What's the matter, Joe?' She could not help herself.

'Nothing.'

'Have I done anything wrong?'

'Not that I know of.'

'Look at me, Joe.'

His jaw muscles tautened the instant before he turned his head.

'Joe.'

'Yes?' The word came out coldly.

'Why are you like this, Joe?'

'Like what?'

He saw her clearly. She stood before him, both hands holding the bag in front of her, her eyes wide and her lips slightly parted. She was like an intensely beautiful child, puzzled but trusting. They were together in a green box made by the hedges that pressed in around them, forced to face each other, and suddenly her beauty was more than he could bear. He had to wound it because it was perfect. His cruelty was white and pure within him. He let it sit in his face.

'Joe?' Her voice was anxious; she was afraid of what she saw. 'Joe?'

'You don't have to repeat my name.'

His victory was instantaneous. She lowered her head, chastised. The blunt toes of her small shoes were pointed together, childishly, and he felt her pain as though it was his own, which it was, and because he needed pain to burn out the anguish and confusion within him his cruelty fed on what it had created.

Her feet scuffed the pebbles of the road and she began, timidly, to back away.

'Goodbye,' he said.

If she replied he did not hear her, but now her back was towards him and she was walking away. He hated her now for leaving him, but savagely he waited for her to turn back of her own accord. All he had to do was to call her name and take a step nearer to shatter his own cruelty and be forgiven, but he held his silence as she took one pace and then another, and he let her get nearer the invisible line that would make calling out or turning back impossible.

He let her go farther and farther until, at the very last instant, he opened his mouth to call.

And then it was too late. A voice from the other direction made him spin round. Ralph, still at some distance from him, stood in the centre of the lane. He shouted Joe's name again and raised a hand in greeting. Joe ignored him and turned quickly, but Jenny was almost out of sight.

'Pity.' Ralph came alongside him and stood looking after her. 'She's the little girl I saw the day we arrived.'

'She told me.'

'You're a lucky devil, Joe, to have her as first reserve.'

Ralph saw the beginning of a frown on Joe's face and grinned. 'Don't worry,' he said, 'the secrets of your love life are safe with me, and that's not what I've come to discuss with you.'

'Thank God for that.' Joe watched until Jenny had vanished around the bend and then he turned and walked back along the lane with Ralph.

'I've been to the workshop,' said Ralph, 'and as you weren't there I had a word with the old gentleman in the cloth cap and he was quite agreeable.'

'To what?'

'A proposition, Joe, to which I hope you will agree. Both of us do, in fact.'

'You and Mr Wilby?' Joe felt his pride touched.

'No, no,' said Ralph hastily. 'Grace and I. We want you.'

Joe waited to be told more.

'Well, not so much me as my mother,' Ralph said. 'You have this extraordinary effect on women.'

Joe shrugged. 'I hadn't noticed.'

'But they are aware of it, Joe. And once Grace had this idea in her head only you would do.'

'What idea is that?'

'That you should be the one to help us out. Decorating; hanging wallpaper and all that.'

Joe looked at him suspiciously, and Ralph laughed.

'The old master at his bench speaks highly of you, Joe, and is willing to release you for as long as it takes.'

It was an escape; he would be out of the village, away from Jenny and all the complexities that pressed on him. 'Well,' he said, 'only if you want to risk it.'

'Not me, Joe boy, so much as Grace. I think it was the sweaty masculinity of your appearance yesterday that tipped the scales.'

FIFTEEN

The sun, low over the horizon, was full in Dot's face as she opened the back door.

'Jenny!' she said. 'I never expected to see you.'

'I had to find somebody.'

'Where's Joe?'

Jenny shrugged, holding herself stiffly, and Dot blamed herself for not detecting at once that something was wrong and that Joe was the cause.

'Come you on in.' She stepped out on to the concrete path to let Jenny go ahead of her into the kitchen, but a child's cry came from somewhere within and then the raised voice of her mother, and Dot clicked her tongue and raised her eyes to heaven, laying a hand on Jenny's arm to prevent her going inside. 'Maybe we're best out of it.' She pulled the door closed. 'But ain't it hot out here?'

The council houses stood on a low rise downstream from the village and almost hidden from it. At the back, their mottled brick was face to face with the sun across the fields.

'Like a bloody oven,' said Dot, but saw immediately that the word did not fit Jenny's mood, and added quickly, 'I'm sorry, Jenny, I didn't ought to have spoken like that.'

'I'm stupid.'

'No, you ain't.' Dot stepped from the concrete to the cinder path that led down the garden. 'Come on.'

She ushered Jenny ahead of her. 'I didn't wait to see you last night when you left to call for Joe.' She cleared her throat saying demurely, 'Ahem,' as a preliminary to adding, 'Because that there Richard wouldn't let me alone for a moment.'

'Wouldn't he?' Jenny did not even turn her head.

'It was embarrassing.' Dot, delighted, would have told her more, but she glimpsed Jenny's pale cheek, as plump as a child's, beyond the smooth edge of the black hair and her sympathy came flooding back. Poor kid, she thought, and when they came to a tier of rabbit hutches that stood against the wall of a shed near the bottom of the garden she stopped as though Jenny was indeed very young and could be distracted like a child.

'Look at him.' Dot pointed as a big white buck, more aggressive than timid, came up to the wire and crouched, watching them with angry pink eyes. Jenny stood solemnly in front of the cage, and Dot rattled her nail against the wire above his head until he raised his nose and sniffed at her finger. 'Randy old devil,' she said to him. 'I know what you want, don't I? But you can't have it because it's rationed.'

In spite of herself Jenny laughed.

'They're all the same,' said Dot, 'men.' But in case she was pressing too soon into Jenny's distress, she added, 'At least the ones I know are.' And then, so that Joe might be excluded, 'Some of them, anyway.'

But Jenny kept her eyes fixed on the hutches and Dot impatiently tugged at her hand and led her round behind the shed to where a plank laid across two logs made a bench. They sat down. Only a ditch separated them from a vast shallow saucer of fields filled to the brim with the golden horizontal light of the sun, and Dot, gazing out across it, shifted slightly on the thick grey wood that all day had absorbed the sun's heat.

'That make you broody,' she said.

'Joe doesn't like me.' Jenny was sitting up straight, her hands grasping the plank at her sides.

'That ain't true!' Dot jerked her head round and her short dark hair made a mesh over her eyes. She pushed it aside. 'Not Diana, is it?' The thought of that night, now long ago with his mother's death between, when Diana had come down to the bridge and taken Joe away had suddenly come into her mind and into her mouth.

'Why should it be Diana?'

'No reason.' Dot spoke hastily, and then thought she had to give an explanation. 'Just that she's always hanging round anything in trousers.' And then, because that did not seem complimentary to Joe, 'But I reckon it's them new people up at the house she's after.'

Jenny did not seem to have heard. 'He hates me.'

Dot saw her, facing the sun, the clear lines of her profile gilded by it with even a glint of gold in the corner of her eye, and a moment's jealousy leapt within her before sympathy smothered it.

'But Joe's a nice old boy,' she said. 'He's ever so gentle.'

'Not to me. Not now.'

'What have gone wrong then, Jen?'

Jenny sat silent.

'Jen.' Dot spoke softly. 'Is it because of his mother?'

Jenny took time to reply, and then she said, almost reluctantly, 'Maybe.'

'It were a shock for him. It'll take time for him to get over it.'

Jenny thought again of the night before Mrs Judd died, the teacups and the little woman's eagerness to talk. 'She knew she was going to die.'

'Jenny!'

'She knew. I think she wanted me to know.'

'Do you think so?' Dot was awed. Their roles seemed suddenly to have changed and it was now Jenny who was the elder.

'It was in everything she told me,' said Jenny, 'but I didn't understand.'

'And Joe? Did he know?'

'It didn't matter what Joe knew.' She was letting her voice drift away as though it dissolved in the light across the field. 'She was sure he was mine.' Her eyes were wide, hypnotized by the sun. 'She gave him to me.'

Jenny paused and Dot waited, unsure of what was happening in the other girl's mind but already half afraid of it. Then Jenny turned away from the sun and she was smiling.

'He doesn't know much, does he?' she said.

'Don't smile like that, Jenny. You give me the creeps.'

'She gave him to me.'

'You look cruel, Jenny.'

'But he hates me.'

'But not for ever. Joe ain't like that.'

'We'll see.'

Jenny took her eyes from Dot and stared out once more over the fields flooded with sunlight. She felt powerful, able to swim in the golden air, and when she smiled Dot shivered and murmured, 'Surely he have suffered enough.'

The rabbit thumped in its hutch behind the shed and at the noise Jenny laughed.

'It's no good,' she called to it over her shoulder, 'didn't you know it was rationed?'

SIXTEEN

'Is that you?'

Grace Jervis opened the bedroom door to step onto the landing as she called out and heard her own voice, loud enough in the bedroom, diminished suddenly by the body of the house.

'Ralph!'

There was no answer and she stepped across the bare boards to speak over the bannister. She had taken off her dress, and in her slip felt the air in the undisturbed centre of the house chill her shoulders.

'I fell asleep,' she called. 'Put the kettle on, would you?'

The window in the bedroom behind her let in a shaft of golden light, but the hall below was already in its own twilight. It remained silent.

'Damn the boy if he won't answer.'

Hugging herself she went back into the room where she was flooded by the horizontal sun.

She shuddered, enjoying the warmth, and suddenly dipped her head sideways until she was biting her own shoulder. She could see herself in the long mirror of the dressing table and for one fleeting moment caught herself off guard. She looked very young. Her shoulder was white and smooth and the face that nestled against it, pink mouth open to show the wet glint of her teeth, was unlined. At least from this distance. She regarded herself from under her thick blonde hair, tousled from the pillow. For a moment she did not look for blemishes and then, before familiarity returned, she let her gaze wander.

The wardrobe door behind her stood ajar but the only dress it revealed was black. It was the one she had worn to the funeral.

'Poor Betty,' she said aloud. 'It's not fair.'

She had lost the desire to look at herself but automatically bent to the mirror to put a finger to each corner of her mouth, smoothing the edge of her lips. The movement of her fingertip in the mirror seemed to be caught and reflected in the window beyond and she let her eyes flicker to it, thinking an insect was crawling on the glass. But what was moving was a distant figure on the long drive curving away through the grass. Very small and bent, but moving away. She drew in her breath sharply. Mrs Goodchild had called while she slept.

Thank God Ralph had been there to get rid of her. But what had she wanted?

Grace went quickly through the open door to the landing and stood listening.

'Ralph!'

She called once more, and again her voice stirred nothing but its own echo, and it was then that she remembered that she was, after all, alone. He had gone to see Joe about helping with the work and must have lingered. The thought of the old woman creeping to the house while she lay unaware and helpless upstairs made her shudder and she took a step towards the bedroom, intending to get dressed. But suddenly she turned away. It was only harming herself to give way to these sensations. To hell with Mrs Goodchild. It was her own house and there was nothing to prevent her moving about in it as she pleased, noisily or quietly, dressed or undressed. She would go downstairs as she was and make herself some tea.

The heels of her shoes clattered on the stairs as she went down. There would be another sound, muffled and rich, when the carpet arrived. Joe would help Ralph to lay it. He was big and capable, and she was pleased she had thought of employing him. She owed it to Betty's memory. But what if they came back while she was dressed like this? She grimaced. Too bad; it was her house and they would have to put up with it.

The hall was warm and full of the grains of twilight and she stood for a moment breathing the dense air. To move through the house almost naked was to take possession of it. It made more sense than signatures.

She began to cross the hall, but at the dining room door a faint sound came to her and she paused. Instantly there was silence. Then she moved again and there was a small, urgent rustle that made her smile. Even her slip echoed in the empty, uncarpeted spaces.

But the dimness had thickened and she spoke aloud. 'I hope he gets back before it's dark.'

This time the sound began before she moved. Her fingers, clutching her upper arms, felt the skin roughen.

'That damned cat!'

Twice, a big stray animal had walked into the house. But it was black; lucky.

'Who let you in this time?'

She opened the door. The room was big and without furniture except for the oval dining table in the middle and six chairs spaced out along the walls.

'Come on out!'

She threw the door wide and stood to one side so that fur would not touch her legs.

Silence.

'Puss!'

A scrabbling in the hearth drew her close to the table. The glossy oval of its polished surface, like a black lake, gathered light and drew it down to its depths.

'Come out!'

She leant over the table to see into the hearth and her reflection floated beneath her, pallid and haggard.

'Puss!' It was almost a shriek.

The black mouth gaped in the marble fireplace. There was a flutter in its throat.

Not a cat.

A great rook, blinded by soot, spread its wings and staggered into the air from the black throat. With the beat of the huge black wings she smelt the stench of soot. It clawed at the air, unable to hold itself, and fell.

She heard its stiff feathers scrape the table. She watched it crouch in the lake. She saw the red mouth open like a wound in the soot. And the wound shrieked.

SEVENTEEN

Joe had found himself in charge soon after Ralph had let him into the house and discovered his mother standing on the landing too afraid to come down until the bird had been taken out. It was Joe who had done it while they watched, and they had been full of gratitude but then, as though everything unpleasant was in bad taste, it had been laughed at and thrust aside.

Joe was glad of it, and glad now, next morning, to be left working alone. It was their tact which had detected that still he found people, even those he enjoyed, too complicated to deal with. In front of him they spoke in flippancies, taking nothing seriously, sailing on the surface of emotions so that whenever his grief returned they helped him to ignore it and it would slide away, subsiding as smoothly as a wave that was given no chance to break.

And now they had left him in the big upstairs room. Its dimensions made it almost a cube, large enough to take a four-poster bed and still leave much space, but filled with nothing now but light. It occupied a corner of the house so that two vast windows in adjoining walls gave it an airiness that seemed almost to make it float free of the house itself, and even the ceiling, an elaborate pattern of foliage in white plaster spreading outwards from the centre, appeared to be resting on nothing but air.

It was a place he would have chosen to work in, and the work was what he needed. Over the years the floorboards had shrunk and some were loose and rattled against the joists and in several places nail heads showed above the wood. He had a punch and hammer and worked methodically along the boards, tapping the nail heads down so they were hidden once again beneath the surface and the boards were firm. He was absorbed in his work and did not hear the heavy door as it swung open, but even so her voice did not startle him.

'Are you at your prayers?'

He was on his knees in a square of sunlight close to a window and he sat back on his heels to see Ralph's mother smiling at him across the room.

'You look like a monk in this bare room,' she said. 'In his cell. No, don't get up.' She closed the door and walked towards the centre of the room, raising her head to look at the ceiling and then at the bare walls. 'Do you like this room, Joe?'

'Very much.'

'I thought you would, but it's more Ralph's taste than mine. Why are you men always so spartan?'

'It's simpler.'

'Nonsense. It makes you concentrate and I don't like that. I like something to distract me. I can't bear simplicity.'

Joe shrugged and smiled at her. He wanted to say that she knew how to make use of simplicity herself, but he knew that to pay her compliments would make him blush. But it was true. She wore a linen dress, tan-coloured and without decoration except for the thin belt that held it in at the waist, and her shoes were a plain network of thin straps. There was a kind of harmony between her and the apparently

99

stark room; neither were as simple as they seemed.

With her head tilted back to examine the ceiling, she said, 'I must thank you for what you did yesterday, Joe.'

'It wasn't much.'

'Wasn't it?' She spoke lightly, looking at him now, but he guessed that it was to talk about the rook that she had come to see him. 'That son of mine couldn't have done what you did.' She was smiling but he saw that she held herself stiffly to prevent a shudder at the thought of the black mass of feathers on the table top.

'It was dead,' he said.

'But how could you bear to touch it?'

He shrugged. 'You just do.' But he knew that it had been because she and Ralph were watching that he had gone straight to the table and thrust his fingers into the cold black heap.

'Well, I think you were brave.' She came closer and looked down at the spot where he was working. 'What are you doing?'

'Punching down nail heads. Some of them are proud. Look.' He reached forward, brushing the boards, just as she stepped nearer and his hand for a split second lay over her bare toes. He snatched it away so sharply that she laughed.

'They won't bite you.'

He was blushing and did not dare look up, but suddenly she crouched and her perfume mingled with the dust in the room.

'Show me what you are doing,' she said.

He put the punch to a nail head and hammered it down.

'And do you have to go over the whole floor like that? One by one?'

'Yes.'

She had forced him to meet her eyes. The blueness was startling and the black pinpoints of her pupils darted and probed into him seeking an answer to a question she had not yet asked. And then her glance fell and for a second he watched her unobserved. The years had only slightly blurred the outlines of her chin and mouth, but he knew they were softer now than when she had been his age. As he watched, her lips opened and he saw the delicate inward skin drawing apart.

'Joe.'

He waited, and when she continued to speak she was regarding the floor.

'I'll tell you something before I tell Ralph. He's bound to tease me and I know you won't. It's about that old woman; Mrs Goodchild.' She raised her head and her attention was full on him now. 'She was here just before that horrible bird got into the house.'

'What did she say?'

'I didn't speak to her. I saw her outside, through the window.'

Suddenly he was back in the cottage with his mother, and the old woman, yellow and wrinkled, stood outside.

'You as well?' he said.

She waited, her mouth open, and he had to tell her more.

'She was the same with my mother,' he said. 'She watched the house.'

She drew in her breath and for three seconds there was silence in the room. And then she said, 'I was going to ask you to do something, Joe, but now I'm not sure that I should.'

'What is it?'

She did not answer him directly. 'We both knew her. Your mother; Betty and me both knew her.'

'I know that.'

She stood up. 'I'm being foolish,' she said. 'I have no right to ask you.'

Joe also got to his feet. 'You'll have to, now,' he said.

She thrust her fingers into her hair and shook her head. 'It's that rook, Joe. It seemed so sinister. And she was there at the same time. I was going to ask you to find out what she wanted, but I can't now.'

'I don't see why not.'

'But not after what you've told me about Betty. It wouldn't be fair.'

'I'll do it for you.'

'Really?' Whatever scruples she had had vanished, and she was smiling at him. 'Are you sure?' He nodded, and she said, 'I'll go with you. I don't mind so long as you are there.'

Joe shook his head. 'It's not necessary.'

'But I must. Please let me, Joe?'

She was pleading and suddenly she was very young.

'All right,' he said. 'When do you want to go?'

'Now?'

He laughed at her eagerness and she coloured slightly.

'Let's go,' he said.

As they left the room she was laughing at herself and him. 'Do you always do just what the girls ask you, Joe?'

'Always.'

'No wonder you are so popular with them.'

'I didn't know I was.'

She gave him a sidelong glance. 'Oh yes,' she said, 'you are more popular than you think.'

EIGHTEEN

It was precisely like a dream, even to the way she recognized it as a dream while it was happening. It was presented to her like a series of painfully bright pictures she had to observe and could do nothing to alter.

There was the car glittering at the corner of the green as she and Dot crossed the bridge. She recognized it, and was warned, but did nothing.

Next, Ralph came out of the shop, not seeing them and, unnecessarily it seemed, threw open a door and the boot one after the other.

And then she and Dot stood still and waited to be seen but, completely dreamlike, were ignored as he leant into the car, disappearing from them behind the seats.

They were several paces nearer when he again came into view. He was preoccupied, busy with something, and he had his lips pressed together as he thought, making his mouth a severe line. He seemed suddenly to hear them and turned with a frown, but the instant he saw them his face changed and the creases deepened in the narrow, lean face as he grinned.

'At last,' he said, and his eyes did not for a moment leave Jenny as he introduced himself.

Dot took it upon herself to tell him their names, but he said 'I know' before she had told him who Jenny was, and Dot doubted whether he heard her own name at all. Strangely, even though Dot made a move to do so, he did not offer to shake hands but stood in front of them wordless and smiling as though, with them, he had been caught within a picture in which nothing would ever move.

He was, or seemed to be, older than Jenny had thought and he appeared to be carelessly dressed in a thin vee-necked pullover without a shirt, and cotton trousers that were obviously not new. Yet he was neat, even fussily so, and the faded beige of the pullover and bleached tan of the trousers could have been arrived at with care. His fair hair had been lightened by the sun, as his skin had been slightly darkened, as though they also had been easily willed into harmony.

'Just wait there.' It was as much an order as a request and made Dot raise her eyebrows at Jenny as he turned and went back into the shop to reappear after a moment laden with tins of paint and rolls of wallpaper. The paint he placed in the boot, and the paper on the back seat. 'It's only lining paper,' he said, 'but one may as well take care of it.'

'One may,' said Dot, mimicking him and hoping to get a giggle from Jenny, but the face framed in the black hair was solemn.

Ralph did not spend time on courtesies. 'So now we have met,' he said, 'come up to the house and meet my mother. Joe is there.'

He walked around the car to open the door for them, and Dot, glancing quickly at Jenny, said, 'Sorry, that's impossible.'

'For both of you?' He looked from one to the other, not bothering to disguise which of them interested him.

'I got a date,' said Dot.

'Which leaves Jenny.' He spoke before Dot could add anything.

The door was open. Without a word, Jenny stepped forward and got in.

'Goodbye then, Jen.' Dot leant forward, trying to catch Jenny's eye, but the car began to move and she failed. She watched it as he eased it around the cottages and out of sight and she murmured to herself, 'Have fun, Jenny, but I hope you know what you're up to.'

'Actually,' said Ralph, 'I lied slightly.'

The car whined in low gear up the hill and Jenny sat, her hands in her lap, gazing straight ahead into the green tunnel of trees.

'Joe is not, at this moment, at the house. Nor is my mother. They are visiting someone in the village.'

Still she did not reply, but she was aware that he did not glance towards her expecting her to say anything.

'I shall go back for them when I have delivered the paint.'

The car came out on to the flank of the hill and drifted along easily until, just before the road dipped down again to go in behind the village, Ralph turned into the entrance of the drive where the new gatepost gleamed. He nodded towards it.

'That's Joe's work.'

'I know.' They were the first words she had said.

'He's a man of many talents.' The car rocked gently, easily smoothing the dips and pockets in the drive, and came out into the open field. 'And very attractive to women. And to me, too.' Ralph, steering with one hand, put his other arm through the open window and patted the roof of the car. A lark suddenly sprang into song above them, its sound quite clear over the engine noise, and Ralph smiled to himself. 'He is big but gentle. Or is that too crude an analysis?'

'Not so gentle.' The wound was still too painful to be forgiven, and she wished for revenge.

Like a man stepping into a crowded lift, Joe edged inside the little cottage and pushed the door closed behind him. They were all three crammed into a narrow passage filled with the musty smell of age. Grace stood directly in front of him and, in front of her but shielded from his sight, the old woman stood mutely regarding them in the dim light.

Suddenly it was difficult to breathe and he twisted his head to look for ventilation, but there was nothing to help him and the women stood where they were, talking now but not moving. He bent his head and found himself examining the carpet that, too wide for the passage, was folded under to make a run for spiders against the skirting board. He closed his eyes and forced himself to breathe slowly.

'This room is too big for you,' said Ralph. 'You look lonely.'

'I'm not.' Jenny had to defy him. He was assessing her against his own background, and she did not want to be examined. 'I'm not lonely at all.' But the room was very large and the furniture was so widely spaced on the plain oiled wood floor that it also seemed to be on display. And the tall windows filled the room with light. It was expensive air and space.

'I'll fetch Joe in a minute,' he said.

'You needn't bother.'

'Poor Joe, I thought you and he were . . .' He left the sentence unfinished but when her only response was to look around the room as though she was in a museum and the chairs were exhibits, he abandoned his oblique questioning, and went on, 'Grace, my mother that is, and he have gone on a quest.'

'A quest?' She made herself sound barely interested.

Ralph smiled. 'It's something that began the day we got here. And you were there, too.'

'How could I have been?'

'It was the first time I saw you. On the village green.'

She remembered; even the fact that she had been picking paint from the seat with her fingernail.

'Mrs Goodchild,' he said. 'That's who they've gone to see.'

'But why her?'

'Because poor Grace is disturbed by her. A figure from the past. But I don't know why that should trouble her. Is there some village mystery that is hidden from me?'

There was distance between them. He stood against one of the windows with his back to the glass almost, it seemed to her, posing with one arm high against the wall. She was near the centre of the room, in open space, forced unwillingly onto a stage.

'There is no mystery that I know of.' She would tell him nothing of the old woman's son or her churchyard visits.

'Well, Joe will put her mind at rest no doubt.'

'No doubt,' said Jenny.

Mrs Goodchild had not yet recognised her. Like a child obeying a stranger she had backed into the cottage as soon as Grace had taken a step towards her, but it seemed that the memory that had brought her out onto the green only days before had faded and vanished.

She stood mumbling in front of them, preventing them from moving, and in desperation Joe had to make something happen. He began to edge past Grace and reached beyond her to the door of the front parlour.

'Can we go in here?' he said and turned the handle.

Obediently she shuffled through into the room and they followed.

'It was the bird.' Ralph's voice was relentless, amused at the sequence of events and assuming that Jenny also would find it entertaining. 'She told me it came down the chimney only a moment after she had seen Mrs Goodchild disappearing in the distance; rather as though they had called on her together.' He laughed. 'To my poor mother's mind, the bird was like a witch's familiar.'

'That's stupid,' said Jenny.

'But that is not all.' It was a game to Ralph and he wanted to extend it. He spoke with detachment, but emphasizing his words. 'At the funeral the old woman smiled at her,' he paused, 'across the grave.'

Jenny had been standing with her hands loosely joined in front of her, but now, to detach herself from him and what he was saying, she raised one arm and, with the back of her hand against her cheek, pushed her hair back until it lay on her shoulder.

'Very pretty,' he said, and she was startled, realizing suddenly that she was still under inspection. But still he did not free her from what he had to say. 'And as Mrs Goodchild smiled, all the rooks came clattering out of the churchyard trees.'

The room was crowded to the walls. High-backed chairs, a horsehair settee and an upright piano with curling brass candle-holders stood against the faded wallpaper, and the empty grate was hidden by a black firescreen on which a barefoot girl ran without moving after a motionless butterfly. On the piano a small transparent dome contained little birds whose colours glinted like broken glass, and the centre of the room was taken up by a red rosewood table that held, stacked one to each corner, four equal piles of gilt-edged books with thick, embossed covers.

They sat and waited for the old opaque eyes that faced them to absorb their images while, above their heads, pictures in heavy frames leant inwards as though they also were watching.

Ralph shrugged himself away from the wall. 'So rooks and Mrs Goodchild obsess her,' he said.

They had their backs to the window and faced Mrs Goodchild across the table. Her small head, the thin hair drawn tightly back, seemed to Joe to shrink until it was an object in the corner of the big coloured print of a battle that hung behind her. It was as rigid as the frightened grey and brown horses that pawed at the smoke over dead soldiers in uniforms of pink and blue, yet suddenly it spoke.

'You wasn't at home.'

Recognition had filtered through, and Joe sensed rather than saw Grace shake her head.

'So you come to see me.'

Grace nodded, and the fragile old head, as brown and wrinkled as dead flowers, nodded with her in the silence. The movement seemed mechanical and Joe noticed that the brooch of garnets at the neck of the old woman's dress did not stir.

'Tom's over there at the side of you.' She had raised her hand, the crooked finger pointing.

They both jerked their heads round but there was nothing beside them save the mantelpiece.

'That's him.'

And then Joe saw the photograph in the middle of the shelf flanked by vases and statuettes.

'You can look at it.'

There could be no disobeying. Joe reached and took it down, glancing at Grace and seeing that she had one fist held to her mouth and was biting the knuckles. He held the photograph so that they could both see it.

A young man stood by a deck-chair in the garden, smiling directly at whoever was holding the camera but with his head tilted slightly towards one shoulder.

'That's a good likeness, ain't it, Gracie?'

It was a pleasant face, innocently beaming, but though the smile was wide the lips were closed as though it was an effort on occasions such as this to contain his excitement. He did not wear a jacket, but his shirt sleeves were buttoned to the wrist and the tie tucked inside the neck of his pullover had his shirt collar pinned tightly beneath it. But none of this was as important as the tilt of his head. For Tom Goodchild leant grotesquely sideways, almost all of his weight supported by a thick walking stick. Joe had not known the most obvious thing about him; he was a cripple.

'Do you remember the rooks at the funeral?' said Ralph.

Jenny shook her head. It was the rook that cried out when Joe's mother ran into the graveyard that filled her mind. The birds seemed to be everywhere, observing what went on below and crying out warnings that nobody heeded.

III

'Well, let's forget all that.' Ralph had come close and she had been so full of her own thoughts that she had not noticed. 'I think it's time we went to fetch them,' he said.

Jenny nodded.

'This way then.' He directed her towards the door, standing back and speaking gently as though he sensed something of what was in her mind. She gave him a half-smile and walked ahead of him towards the door.

Joe held out the photograph but Grace sat with both hands clenched in her lap and made no move to take it.

'Put it back.' She spoke without taking her eyes from Mrs Goodchild. 'Please put it back.' Her voice was insistent.

Mrs Goodchild seemed to notice nothing. 'He was always fond of you two girls.' The old head was nodding with pride and smiling. 'Many's the time I see his face light up when you two came by.'

Grace interrupted abruptly. 'I think it's time for us to go.'

'Nobody were as nice to him as you two girls. I used to sit him out in the sunshine against the front step and there he would stay and watch for you hours on end.'

Grace was unable to remain in the room much longer. She bit the corner of her mouth, frowning at being unable to penetrate the old woman's mind and make her release them.

'He would rattle with his stick and laugh and clap his hands when you two was in sight. I always knew.'

And suddenly Joe realized what caused the innocence in Tom Goodchild's face. It was more than his body that had been crippled.

Ralph reached ahead of Jenny to turn the door handle and their arms touched. He could have taken advantage of it and she hesitated, head bowed, as though she expected it, but he opened the door wide and stood back.

'Thank you.' She glanced up at him.

He was smiling. 'Don't mention it.'

The old woman cackled. The thin sound issued from her and lay in the air between them, and through it Joe reached forward to replace the photograph.

'I told him you was come back, Gracie. I told him both his girls was together again. But he knew all along. He said it were going to happen long before it did. He were a clever boy.'

From the corner of his eye Joe saw Grace's hands unclench and dart quickly to her sides as she prepared to stand up, but the voice did not cease.

'He only wanted to see you both together again. That's all.' She paused, chewing. 'He have seen the other one. He have seen Betty.'

Grace was on her feet with Joe beside her, but the opaque eyes seemed to have seen nothing move.

'One night she come to see him, but you wasn't there and you was the one he wanted most of all. That's all he want now; to see his Gracie. You was always his favourite.'

Slowly Joe began to edge around the table.

'That's all he want now. He have never settled. He have never been at peace; never since that night.'

Grace drew in her breath sharply and the sound penetrated the old mind.

'He never could bear to see anyone suffer; if a child did but cry his eyes was full of tears. He think you might be miserable, Gracie, after what he done.'

Her words stopped, but they knew there was more to come. She had a message to deliver, and she seemed to be listening as she spoke.

'He say he'll be there again. At the place where you was to meet. He'll be there when the time come.'

Joe put himself between her and Grace as she fell silent. No more words came as they reached the door, and the eyes that were directed at them as they left the room were as blind as marble.

Jenny waited, standing by the open door, until he could not mistake what she intended, and when he kissed her she was fierce.

NINETEEN

'Hide me,' said Jenny.

'You can stay here as long as you like.' Dot lifted the tiny brown rabbit up to her face and spoke to it. 'Can't she?' she said. 'She can hide away from that big handsome feller just as long as she like.'

'Give it to me.' Jenny reached out and Dot put the little creature into her hands. It was very soft, but under its fur she could feel its fragile bones. She put it in her lap. 'There now,' she said. 'You'll be safe there.'

'Or as my Richard say when I do that,' said Dot, 'lucky little bunny.'

Jenny bent her head over it. Its ears lay along its back like the wings of sycamore seeds but softer than velvet. It was trembling and she made a ring with her arms to encircle it. 'I wish it was mine,' she said.

'You can have it,' said Dot.

'No, I don't mean that. I wish it was really mine. My own little baby bunny.'

Dot, on the bench beside her, leant over and scratched the little rabbit between the ears. 'Do you hear that?' she said. 'Jenny wants to be your mummy. Aren't you a lucky little bunny?'

'You frighten him.'

Dot took her hand away. 'All right, mummy bunny,' she said.

'Stop it.' Jenny looked up.

Dot met her eyes and held them. 'It's still Joe, isn't it?'

'No.'

'That's not the truth.'

'It is,' said Jenny. 'That's finished with and I'm glad.'

'You can't be.'

'I am.'

'But his mum was so fond of you.'

'That's why I'm so glad it's over. I'm sick and tired of his mother.'

Dot sighed and was silent for a moment. Then she said, 'Do you like this Ralph?'

'Of course I do.'

'Why are you hiding from him, then?'

'Because I'd rather be on my own.'

Dot leant over and again touched the little rabbit's head. 'We don't all understand your mummy,' she said, 'but maybe she knows what she's doing.'

Jenny said nothing, but the silence was broken by Dot's mother calling from the house behind them. Dot went to the path at the side of the hutches.

'What is it?' she shouted.

'Somebody to see Jenny.'

They exchanged glances. 'Oh hell,' said Dot, 'he's found you.'

'I know.'

Jenny stood up and Dot, as she took the rabbit from her, said, 'You ain't going, are you?'

'Yes.'

Her calmness alarmed Dot and she said, 'Well, I'm coming as well.'

'Please yourself.'

Dot stooped, holding the little rabbit against her face before she put it back in the hutch, and she murmured, 'You'll be safe in there while I see that mummy bunny don't get into no trouble.' She expected a smile from Jenny but, when she straightened, Jenny had her back to her and was already moving away.

TWENTY

Ralph had stopped on the bridge to pick up Diana. There was no polite way of avoiding it after she had waved to the other two girls, but now, in the house, she was doing her best to monopolize him.

She was coy. 'When you go back to university,' she said, 'what will you tell them about us?'

'I shall tell them of your sophistication, of course.'

'Sophistication!' Diana gave a little shriek and for almost the first time looked at Jenny and Dot, as though both were good examples of the lack of it.

'Diana,' Ralph brought her attention back to himself. 'You are sophisticated because you all appear so calm.'

Diana sat wide-eyed, admiring him and ready to be instructed. He grimaced slightly, not wanting the role of instructor thrust on him, but went on, 'There is more going on under the surface here than in any place I have ever been.'

'You surprise me,' said Diana, demonstrating that emotion.

'Do I really?' He spoke so off-handedly that Dot thought Diana must surely see she was being snubbed, but she merely wriggled in her chair and said, 'What can you have found out?'

They were in the kitchen making coffee and he went to the dresser in the corner, got some cups and brought them back to the table before he leant towards her and said, 'For one thing, I know something about you.'

'Oh!' Pleased, she put her fingertips to her mouth. 'Nothing bad, I hope.'

'Not bad,' he said, 'but dangerous.'

He spoke so seriously that she had second thoughts and her pale face became paler. 'Dangerous?' she asked, subdued.

'Yes,' he said, 'anybody as attractive as you must be dangerous.'

Her colour changed suddenly and she was blushing against her will. 'Is that all?'

'It's quite enough.' If he had intended to say more he had now changed his mind for he turned away to help Jenny make the coffee.

Dot was uncomfortable and shy, but this seemed only to have heightened her observation. She could not prevent herself studying Diana. It was the hands that gave her away. They were long and almost plump; certainly they carried more flesh than the rest of her, and Dot wondered how she could be as proud of them as she obviously was when they were so large and deathly white. But she constantly used them, gesturing, drawing objects in the air with a fingertip or shaping invisible objects with smooth, plump palms; or, worst of all, while some other person was speaking, she would let them dance on a chair arm, slide along a hem, trace a pattern, pick at a thread, kiss each other, flutter, wink, bow, stoop, lie on their backs with their legs in the air like white crabs, or touch each other between the fingers and sniff and giggle like a pair of disgusting and precocious children whose mother refused to correct them. But then, like such children, they would let her down, saying more about her than she wished, stripping her as naked as they were themselves.

Their betrayal began early. As soon as Ralph turned away from her towards Jenny, the hands curled, nails inwards, until they bit themselves cruelly.

Ralph was checking the cups. 'There's four of us here,' he said, 'and Joe and Grace.'

'Grace?' Diana seized at any chance to keep the conversation.

'My mother; but still recognized hereabouts as Gracie Jervis.'

'Of course!' said Diana. 'But isn't she lovely!'

'You've seen her?'

Diana smiled. 'Everybody was talking about her at the funeral.' At the word, Diana stopped with a little gasp and once more her fingers flew to her lips as though she had blundered embarrassingly. 'I'm so sorry, Jenny. I shouldn't have mentioned it.'

It was subtle, yet obvious, this way of connecting Jenny with Joe through the death of his mother, but if it had been intended to throw Ralph into confusion it failed.

'Grace saw you too, Diana,' he said. 'In a little black hat.'

His smile distanced her, but Diana was an expert at turning aside veiled criticisms. With a kind of girlish vagueness she said, 'But where is Joe?'

'With my mother,' Ralph replied. 'He has become her protector.'

'Ralph!' she cried. 'What can you mean?'

'Something less than you do, I imagine.'

Dot listened and watched and saw that Diana had met her match. Jenny's face through all this was expressionless. She was ignored like Dot herself while the other two sparred.

Ralph was pouring coffee, and Diana saw, as he

plainly intended she should, that the smile that
deepened the vertical creases in his cheeks meant
mischief.

'Now, Ralph,' she said, playfully scolding him,
flirting with him despite Jenny, 'what's going on in
your mind?'

'Grace and Joe,' he said. 'They amuse me. They are
like two children frightened by an old witch. Milk?'
He held a jug over Diana's cup but she shook her head.
'The very sight of old Mrs Goodchild makes both of
them tremble – Grace at least; I can't imagine Joe
exactly trembling, but he displays a kind of apprehen-
sion.' He was looking at Jenny as he spoke, and he
added, 'The old lady talks to her dead son, I believe.'

'Don't.' Jenny's voice was very soft.

'And little Jenny trembles too,' he said. 'But all
that the old lady has done is to tell her poor Tom's
grave that Gracie Jervis has returned.'

'How do you know that?' Jenny said.

'Joe told us. Rather touching I thought it.'

'I love a ghost story!' Diana's hands were pressed
flat together beneath her chin as though for prayer.
'Do tell me more!'

But at that moment the door opened and Ralph's
mother came in followed by Joe. There was, Dot
thought, something faintly regal about them, a sense
that beyond the walls of the house there was a limitless
kingdom for which they were responsible.

'Is the room finished?' Ralph asked them.

'Almost,' said his mother.

'And the decorations, are they a success?'

Grace smiled at him. 'He is not satisfied but I think
they are perfect.'

'That's Joe; hard to please, hard to get.'

As Ralph handed him a cup, Dot noticed for the

first time that Joe had lost some weight since his mother's death and there was, she thought, still a hint of feverish anxiety in his otherwise gentle eyes. It kept him apart from the rest of them and in a sense it made it easy for him to ignore Jenny and easier for her to be in his company. But Ralph was introducing his mother to herself and Diana.

'You must call her Grace,' he said.

'They may not like to.' Surprisingly, his mother seemed shy.

'I'll call you Grace.' It was Diana who spoke and Ralph, standing close to her, put an arm on her shoulder.

'Nice,' he said satirically, 'isn't that nice?' But his mother's awkwardness had made a gap in the conversation that was only broken when he gently pushed Diana in Joe's direction and said, 'Grab that manly frame and make him steer you towards some sustenance for us all.'

'Manly frame!' Diana, realizing that making up to Joe at this moment would aid her flirtation with Ralph, stepped forward and one of her hands leapt, nimble as a monkey, to his wrist and held him. 'You have to lead me somewhere.'

Joe walked with her towards the dresser from which he reached down a biscuit tin.

'He knows where everything is,' said Ralph. 'He's one of the family. Knows all the family secrets already, don't you, Joe?'

'It's empty.' Joe held up the tin, and Ralph laughed.

'Subject closed,' he said. 'He's very discreet, aren't you, Joe?'

'Not that I'd noticed,' said Joe.

'Oh, but you are.' Ralph was obviously intending to

say more and Dot waited to hear Mrs Goodchild mentioned again, but he had a different mischief in mind. 'Joe knows many things that happen by moonlight and in the long grass.'

Diana suddenly tittered. Her hand flew to her mouth, hid her eyes, perched on her nose and eventually fluttered across to Joe where it hovered over his arm and then alighted there like a white dove. It was a usual attention-getting display, but Grace cut almost brutally across it.

'We intend to have that grass cut, don't we, Joe?' she said.

He nodded. 'Where are the rest of the biscuits?' He stepped forward, leaving Diana alone beside the dresser.

It was cruel the way that he and Grace had seemed to act together against Diana, and suddenly Dot was sorry for her.

TWENTY-ONE

'Your father's got no sense.' Jenny's mother stooped to the little back window to look along the cinder path towards the chicken run. 'What did he want to take him out there for?'

'Oh, Mum,' said Jenny, 'isn't he ever going to bring him in?'

Ralph, much taller than her father, was taking a studious interest in the chickens.

'Once your father gets talking about them birds . . .' said her mother.

'Those birds.'

Jenny's correction came out before she could stop it and she waited tensely for the reaction. But her mother smiled. 'All right,' she said. 'Those birds.'

'I'm sorry, Mum.' Jenny knew that her face was rigid and red and she could not meet her mother's eyes.

'There's nothing to be sorry for,' said her mother, comforting her.

'I never expected him to bring me home,' said Jenny. 'I had to ask him in, hadn't I?'

'And now you're all of a flutter. I know how you feel, my duck.'

'I'm not ashamed or anything.' Jenny was speaking wildly, confused in her own mind but determined, somehow, not to hurt her mother. 'It's just that . . . Oh, I don't know. He's so different.'

'He seems very nice. He was ever so polite, and that pleased your father.'

Jenny nodded.

There was a pause during which her mother stood in front of her and seemed to doubt whether she should ask what was in her mind. And then she decided.

'What about Joe?' she asked.

Jenny found herself, to her surprise, hanging her head like a child. 'That's over,' she said.

Once again the silence hung between them, but the instant before Jenny raised her head her mother spoke.

'I see,' was all she said, but as Jenny opened her mouth to explain that it had been Joe's fault and not hers that they were no longer together, she shook her head and prevented Jenny saying anything at all. And suddenly Jenny wanted to cry, but her mother did not let the moment linger.

'Now what you want to do,' she said, taking her by the shoulder and turning her towards the door, 'is to go upstairs and have a wash and put on something fresh.' She went back to the window and pushed aside the net curtain. 'Damn the man. What does he want to hang about just there for?'

Jenny's father had crouched almost at Ralph's feet to show him some plant growing close to the privy door.

'That man!' Mrs Briggs smoothed her hair and tucked her blouse more neatly into the top of her skirt. 'Just you go on and get changed and I'll shift them away from there.'

Ralph stayed to tea, and Jenny gradually saw that one other thing that her mother had instantly noticed was true. Ralph and her father were very much alike.

Both were lean-faced and both had a kind of fastidious plainness in the way they dressed that showed even in her father's working clothes that he refused to change, despite his wife's plea, because he had to go out later on to do more work that evening. And he and Ralph were similar in a less superficial way. Neither could be embarrassed in conversation.

'Grace Jervis,' said Mr Briggs reflectively, 'or whatever her married name may be.' He glanced at Ralph, but Ralph shrugged as though his mother's name was an irrelevance, and Mr Briggs went on, 'Grace Jervis was always a striking looking girl. I remember her well. Every man of my age would.'

'Hark at Father,' said his wife, 'I wonder what he'll come out with next.'

Jenny's brothers had looked in, eaten quickly and disappeared, leaving their elders when tea was finished to move into the front room where the three-piece suite bulged out from the walls and took up so much of the floor that Ralph's long legs almost touched the neat, small feet of Mr Briggs.

Ralph said to him, 'So you have memories of Gracie Jervis.'

'So it seems,' said Mrs Briggs, and Jenny, sitting beside her on the sofa, pushed her fist into her mother's leg and hoped that she would change the subject.

'Your father,' Mrs Briggs looked indulgently towards her husband, 'has always had an eye for a pretty girl.'

Mr Briggs was not to be deterred. 'There was never anything between me and Grace Jervis,' he said, quite seriously.

'Not through want of trying, I'll be bound,' said his wife, still trying to make light of it.

'Ah.' He considered the matter. 'She was pretty

enough to make me think about it.' He turned to
Ralph. 'She's a good-looking woman now, I dare
say.'

'I believe so.' Ralph was quite unperturbed.

Mr Briggs pursed his lips and nodded. 'Difficult for
you to say, of course, being so close.'

'You'll embarrass the boy,' said Mrs Briggs, 'going
on like that about his mother.'

Mr Briggs had Jenny's clear grey eyes. They could
stare without showing any emotion and did so now as
he lay back, his thick-fingered hands spread on the
rough material of the chair arms on either side of him,
and gazed, mildly enough, at his daughter and then
back to Ralph.

'You have something of your mother in you,' he
said to Ralph. 'Makes you as attractive to a girl, I
dare say, as she was to a man.'

'Honestly!' Mrs Briggs cried. 'Who's going to stop
the man! On and on about everybody's love life, his
own in particular.'

'Now you're talking nonsense, Mother.' He rested
his head on the back of the chair and spoke mildly,
holding them all, like an audience, with his steady
eyes. 'There was never anything between Grace Jervis
and me, and I'll tell you why. Grace Jervis belonged
to a different class.'

Jenny wished him dead and herself with him and
the house burned down on top of them.

'Father!' cried Mrs Briggs.

He turned calmly to Ralph. 'It's true,' he said.

'Then I am pleased those days are over,' said Ralph.

Mrs Briggs' attempt at tact was much clumsier.
'The only classes I knew about in the village,' she said,
'were in school.'

At this, Mr Briggs gave a little laugh and Jenny

prayed that his terrifying determination to be honest would, just this time, permit him not to explore the subject. Her prayer seemed to be answered.

'School,' he said. 'I wasn't in her class there, either. Don't forget I'm a good deal older.'

'That you're not!' His wife was indignant. 'She's only my age.'

'Yes, my dear, but three years is a big gap when you're at school.'

'It didn't stop you getting to know me.'

His expression as he faced his wife was affectionate, but before they could continue talking about their youth, Jenny seized her chance. 'I think it's about time we went,' she said.

Ralph, however, did not stir. It was as though he was in collusion with her father to embarrass her.

'You would know a great deal about my mother that she has never told me,' he said.

'Quite likely.' Mr Briggs gave a little snort of laughter, as though Ralph's outspokenness was too much even for him, and Mrs Briggs broke in.

'But if you think he's going to give away her secrets,' she said, 'you are quite mistaken. I shan't let him.'

Ralph laughed. 'There'll always be a lot I don't know about Grace,' he said.

'What a way to talk about your mother.' Mrs Briggs, fully aware of Ralph's charm and the attitudes he had that differed from her own, nevertheless chided him.

'Don't worry, Mrs Briggs,' he said, 'all I want to know is why my mother still clings to a childish fear of Mrs Goodchild. It seems to have blighted her return'.

The mild grey eyes of Mr Briggs looked at him without understanding, and Jenny was aware that

128

her mother had suddenly ceased her habit of smoothing her skirt over her knees.

Ralph said, 'Unless, of course, it is too scandalous to mention.'

'Of course not,' said Mrs Briggs. 'There was nothing like that.'

But her tone was an admission that something had happened in the past, and Ralph seemed determined to make it impossible for her to refuse to tell him more.

'Joe's mother was involved,' he said, encouraging her to continue.

That Ralph, of all people, should mention Joe made the blood sing in Jenny's ears and she glanced guiltily at her mother, but neither her mother nor anybody else was paying her any attention. It was her father who broke the silence.

'Now you mention it,' he said to Ralph, 'I remember those two girls were always together. Isn't that so, Mother?'

His wife nodded curtly and Jenny could see that she wanted him to stay silent, but he continued, 'Although why they should be afraid of old Mrs Goodchild, I don't know.' He thought for a moment, and then added, 'Unless it was something to do with poor Tom.'

Mrs Briggs began to pat her knees, trying to think of something to say that would change the subject, but Ralph prevented her.

'Tom Goodchild died very young, didn't he?' he said. 'He seems a tragic figure to me.'

Mr Briggs nodded gravely, closing his eyes as he did so, and saying, 'He was. Very tragic.'

'He was never right in the head.' Jenny's mother was brutal. They turned to her, surprised, but she was determined that nobody should feel sympathy for the dead boy. 'There was always something wrong with him or he wouldn't have done what he did.'

'That may be so, Mother,' Jenny's father was replying to her before Ralph was able to ask any questions, 'but he was very fond of those girls.'

'Fond! He plagued the life out of them.'

'Maybe so.' Mr Briggs paused, and Ralph was able to ask his question.

'What happened?' he said.

'Betty told me,' said Mrs Briggs, and then, for Ralph's benefit, added, 'That's Joe's mother.'

'I know.' He nodded. 'Grace calls her Betty.'

'Did she tell you that they had promised to meet him that night?'

He shook his head. 'What night?'

'The night he died, of course. He had been pestering them so much they promised to meet him. It was always your mother he was wild about, not Betty so much.'

'She led him on, I suppose.' The creases deepened suddenly in Ralph's cheeks as though the whole story amused him.

'Betty never said so.' Jenny's mother was deadly serious. 'She blamed herself, poor thing, just as much as Grace.'

'Blamed herself for what?'

'They didn't go.' She looked down into her lap and tightened her skirt savagely over her knees. 'That part of it never came out at the inquest but Mrs Goodchild knew.'

'Inquest?' Ralph's smile had, at last, gone.

She did not raise her head and her lips were tightly sealed. It was left to Mr Briggs to answer.

'On poor Tom,' he said.

'What happened to him?'

'They found him next morning.'

'Where?'

'On top of the hill.'

'You mean above our house?' Ralph was a shade too eager, sensing a good village story.

Mr Briggs looked down at the carpet as though now, for the sake of decency, he wanted to finish this discussion.

'He was a cripple,' he said. 'It was a wonder he got that far.'

'And it was too much for his heart?'

'No!' Jenny heard herself cry out and saw all heads turn towards her. 'He hanged himself. Everybody knows that.'

TWENTY-TWO

'Everything echoes in this house. Have you noticed that?'

'Because it's still empty,' said Joe.

Grace Jervis stood on the curve of the stairs looking down at him. 'It's like living in a great sea shell,' she said. 'It whispers at you all the time.'

The banister on which her hand rested ended in a scroll at the bottom beside Joe. He spread his fingers on the polished, motionless whorl. 'But you're not frightened any more, are you?' he asked. The rook and Mrs Goodchild lingered.

For a moment she did not answer, and then she said, 'Sometimes I think I ought to leave; go away and not come back.'

Her voice was quiet and stirred no echoes.

'But you won't.' He willed her to look at him, but her glance wandered at random through the empty spaces of the hall. 'You've only just arrived,' he said. He put his finger to the bridge of his glasses and the movement brought her eyes down to him.

'It's difficult to come back, Joe. It's like leading a double life.'

'But you can do it.'

'Can I?'

Her scent reached him through the grains of the air.

'Yes,' he said.

'Well, if you say so.' She smiled and began to come down, but, still two or three steps from him, she paused. He saw her shudder.

'It's terrible,' she said.

'What is?'

'Everything.' She curled her fingers tightly closed and, with the soft edge of her fist, gently tapped the banister. 'I'm trapped. Everything is exactly the same as it was and yet it's different. I feel like a ghost.'

'But you aren't.'

She was still for a moment and then she smiled at him.

'I'm not a ghost, am I? Not to you, Joe.'

'No.'

He put a foot on the bottom stair but withdrew it as she descended. He left his hand on the bulging swirl of wood but her fingers stopped just short of it.

'You remind me . . .' she began and then broke off.

'What of?'

'Oh, many things.'

She stood on the bottom stair and her head was level with his. He saw her lips part slightly and suddenly she seemed afraid or confused. 'I'd forgotten how tall you are,' she said, and turned her head away.

'I can't help it.'

The absurd apology made her laugh and she turned back in time to see him, embarrassed, press a finger once again to the bridge of his glasses. 'And you needn't worry about them,' she said. 'They're part of your charm.'

He wanted to touch her but dared not. She stepped down and her eyes flickered up at him and then away, and slowly her hand withdrew from the bannister, drawing threads of sensation from him.

'It is terrible,' she said, 'to find oneself behaving like this.'

She moved away from him in the dim light of the hall. He let her go and she knew he did not follow. The distance between them stretched until, at breaking point, she paused, and he began, then, to move towards her.

'Joe.' Her voice made him hesitate. 'Tell me one thing.'

He waited, behind her back.

'Did Betty,' she said, 'did your mother ever say anything about Tom Goodchild?'

'Not very much. He hanged himself. Out there.' He nodded to where they both knew the hill rose above the house.

'Did you know when it was?' Her eyes searched him.

'No, I don't think so.'

'It was now, Joe. This time of the year. Midsummer Eve.'

She waited, but he had nothing to say.

'I wondered,' she said, and bit her lip. 'I wondered if anything happened then. You know, anything like a ghost. Have there been any stories? You know how things begin and that old woman the other day said he hadn't forgotten, so I wondered . . .'

She was facing him now, raising her hand to her mouth, but he grasped her wrist.

'No,' he said. 'Nothing. Nothing like that.'

'Because we knew him. We knew him.'

'Mrs Goodchild is mad.' Joe's calmness surprised himself. 'And so was her son.'

He felt the tension in her wrist ease.

'Yes, Joe,' she said quietly. 'Yes.'

'And I will not let her harm you.'

She had bowed her head, and now she looked up like a shy girl. She was even smiling, ashamed of her outburst.

'You have protected me already,' she said. 'Without you I could not have remained here.'

The smile on her lips was so faint that the dim light gradually corroded it and, as it faded, silence flooded the hall and drowned his own breathing. It was long ago; far away in a distant land. His eyes were closed and his lips touched hers.

She whispered, and her breath touched his skin. 'You are to blame.'

And then, from far away, the sound came. Wordless. Just a sound in the air.

Her eyes, suddenly, were in the present. 'What's that?'

'I didn't hear anything.'

'Listen!'

Overhead, one rook called to another.

'A rook,' he said.

'It's her, Joe!'

'No!'

'It's her!'

The outer door rattled. Her nails dug into his hand. Voices came from the kitchen. And laughter. Young voices. Ralph had returned.

Grace thrust him from her, and a moment later was running upstairs, leaving him to face the newcomers alone.

TWENTY-THREE

'Still here?' Ralph was surprised when Joe came into the kitchen from the hall.

'I was just on my way,' said Joe.

'There is one on the green who will be glad to know it.'

'Who's that?'

Jenny, half hidden behind Ralph, watched the Rameses lips frame the question and realized, with a tiny leap of excitement, that he did not know who Ralph meant.

'Diana, my boy.'

'Oh.'

'Diana the huntress, chaste and fair. Chased, any-way, through the long grass.'

Joe did not reply. He stood tensely at the corner of the table as though still shy in Ralph's house, and Ralph, sensing Joe's mood, changed the subject.

'Where's Grace?'

'Upstairs, I think.'

'Because we have something to tell her.' He turned to Jenny, smiling. 'Secrets from the past.'

'Don't,' said Jenny. 'Please don't.'

'She will be amused, I promise you.' He put his shoulders against the dresser and folded his arms. 'But from what we hear from Jenny's father I wonder if it's safe for a young fellow to be alone with her.'

He was mocking, but Joe coloured.

'He blushes. And now he turns pale. Is this another candidate for the hilltop?'

Jenny's eyes implored Ralph to stop, but he was getting too much pleasure from the situation to heed her.

'Did you know, Joe, the secret of my mother's past? Why old Mother Goodchild has such a hold over her?'

Joe shrugged. His mouth was too dry to speak.

'Because my mother, Joe, when a girl, helped break poor Tom's heart.'

Jenny murmured something that neither of them could catch.

'What was that?' Ralph moved closer but she merely stared at him, saying nothing but holding his eyes until, suddenly, it dawned on him that Joe's mother was involved in the story.

'Oh.' He paused, raised a hand to the top of his head and slid it down until it was gripping the back of his neck. Then he laughed. 'But that was long ago and far away. It can hurt no one now.'

'It can,' she said.

'Well, not Grace. It will release her from her fears when she hears that I know.' He moved towards the door but hesitated there. 'Don't worry, Jenny, nothing will happen.'

He went out and they were alone together for the first time since the rift between them.

'What was all that about?' Joe heard his own voice break the silence and it sounded brutal, but Jenny's reply was mild.

'Don't pay any attention to him, Joe.'

'Why not?'

'Because he is only going to hurt people, spreading that story around.'

'How is that?'

She did not answer, and they realized together that both of them were tracing patterns on the table with their fingertips. Joe withdrew his hand.

'What was it you found out?' he said.

'Only something that I knew all along. Your mother told me most of it.' She remembered the afternoon of the teacups, and tears came to her eyes.

'About Tom Goodchild?' He forced her to continue.

'They both knew him, Joe. Your mother and Grace Jervis. He pestered them; she told me so.'

He nodded, seeming to know as much as she did.

Jenny bowed her head and again watched her fingers drawing on the table as she spoke. 'I know it wasn't your mother who promised to meet him that night he killed himself on the hill. It was Grace Jervis, I know that, but your mother always blamed herself for not stopping it. She told me so. It plagued her all those years.'

She looked up and saw that his face was blank, not understanding, but then there came a glint of anger from behind his spectacles.

'That damned Mrs Goodchild!' he said softly. 'She tormented my mother and now she's tormenting the other one.' Still he did not mention Grace by name.

'She's harmless, Joe.' Jenny tried to diminish his ferocity. 'She's just a poor old woman.'

'She made my mother miserable.'

'No, Joe. Not at the end. She was not afraid of Tom Goodchild or anything to do with him. You helped her that night.'

'What night?'

'Just before she . . . Oh Joe, surely you remember.'

He was looking at her intensely, waiting for an explanation.

138

'You were in the churchyard,' she said. 'I saw you beckon to her.'

He shook his head.

'But I saw you. You wanted her to go and listen at Tom Goodchild's grave like you did with me, and she went to you. It put her mind at rest, Joe. She saw there was nothing to be afraid of.'

'I was never there.'

'You were.'

'No!'

'But there was someone, Joe. At first I thought it was . . .'

He drew back. 'What are you trying to say?'

'Nothing.' But the hideous possibility had returned. It was not Ralph; she knew that. And it was not Joe.

'You're trying to say she really did see Tom Goodchild?'

In the onslaught of his anger she shook her head.

'You believe it!' he accused her. 'You made it bad for her and now you're making it bad for someone else!'

'No!' She wanted to tell him of the final afternoon when his mother and herself had understood each other and understood Joe, too, without once mentioning the figure that Jenny had seen in the graveyard. 'No,' she repeated. 'Don't go.' But he was already moving towards the door.

'Tell them I'll be back tomorrow,' he said. He had to get out. Away from all of them. He slammed the door and cut off Jenny's useless words.

TWENTY-FOUR

Joe's sudden departure the evening before was not mentioned when, next morning, he returned to the house to continue with the work. It was as though the previous day had never existed, sealed behind the glaze of their immense tact. Ralph joked, making fun of him often but always deferring to him in practical matters, and Grace did not by the slightest glance or gesture indicate that he was to her any more than her son's friend. But yesterday she had seemed very young, and today he saw the wrinkles at the corners of her eyes and the tiny creases at the edge of her mouth, and his shame turned into disgust against her and against himself and he worked with a feverish energy to scour it from his mind.

And yet she was beautiful. Her age made her more than beautiful. It took her beyond the attainable, so that those calm eyes, having seen that he yearned, seemed to him now to regard him with a wistful pity.

He would finish his work and be gone. He was dazzled as he came out of the house holding in both arms a big bundle of damp wallpaper he had stripped from another room upstairs, and he was forced to close his eyes against the white sun that put a silvery bleach on the leaves and grass. He was glad to be alone for a moment and let himself relax as though he floated in the pink warmth behind his eyelids.

Ralph's voice, above and behind him, said, 'I've been here before.'

Joe, still hugging the paper, turned his head to look over his shoulder. Ralph was at the upstairs window of the room he had just left, and Grace was with him.

'Your naked back,' said Ralph. 'That is to blame.'

Joe put the bundle down. He was stripped to the waist and he brushed specks of paper and flecks of paint from his chest and stomach as he tilted his face up to them. 'To blame for what?' he said.

'I suddenly felt all of this had happened before.' Ralph swept his arm in a gesture to take in the paved area on which Joe stood and the grass beyond. 'And now I realize it has. You were hugging a gatepost when we met.'

'Sling down my shirt,' said Joe. 'I've finished.'

It was Grace who picked his shirt from the floor and let it flutter down to him.

As Joe tucked the shirt into his belt, Ralph said, 'All we need now is a lark up there. Remember?'

Instinctively they all looked up, squinting against the sun, but all they saw was a lazy rook swimming across the sky.

'Some bloody lark,' said Joe.

Ralph laughed and turned to his mother. 'He's always the same,' he said. 'He deflates me.'

She did not answer, and Joe finished buttoning his shirt as Ralph went on, still speaking to her but intending Joe to hear, 'Just listen to what he says when I tell him what day it is.'

'Don't, Ralph.' Grace spoke for the first time, and her voice had urgency in it, but Ralph was launched and would not be stopped. He leant a little further from the window and spoke to Joe.

'She has just asked me not to leave her tonight, and do you know why?'

Joe shook his head.

'Because it is Midsummer Eve.'

Grace had been regarding her son, but even as he spoke the blue eyes drifted from him and hesitantly sought Joe. They were very young again and the expression in them asked for his help, but he did not know why.

'She is afraid to be alone.' Ralph was not unkind, but his mother began to draw back into the room as though he caused her pain. 'Midsummer, Joe. Does that mean something special to a countryman?'

Joe sought to keep Grace in view as he replied. 'It means it's bloody hot,' he said.

'You see.' Ralph, laughing again, spoke to his mother. 'He deflates me. Every time. Or else,' he turned back to Joe, 'he keeps me out of some secret known only to you country people.'

Behind him, in the dimness of the room, Grace retreated.

TWENTY-FIVE

The car slid down through the leafy tunnel, its engine
barely audible, as Ralph let it be drawn like a falling
stone into the village.

'There's no need for me to be with you,' Grace said.
'You could do this yourselves.'

'We would forget something, wouldn't we, Joe?'

'I expect so.' Joe was alone in the back.

'But honestly, Joe.' Impulsively Grace turned to
him, putting her elbow over the back of the seat. She
had changed. She was almost flippant again. 'He's
mad to want to hold a party just because it's Midsummer Eve.'

Neither of them had asked him, but both assumed
he would be there.

'It's not as though the house is ready, is it?' she
said.

'Pay no attention to her, Joe. She badly needs male
company on a night like this.'

'Oh, do I?' She spoke with mock indignation.

'Yes, indeed,' said Ralph. 'Even Joe can see that.'

'Joe knows nothing about it.' But, facing him, her
eyelids drooped and she traced a seam in the seat
cover with her fingertips before she turned away and
looked ahead again.

The swish of the car echoed back through the open
windows as they rounded the row of cottages and
emerged at the edge of the green. Ralph eased it into

a patch of gravel near the bridge and switched off.

'Well?' said Grace as he sat with his hands on the steering wheel, making no attempt to get out of the car.

'It's happened again.'

'What has?'

'I've been here before. Look.'

He was facing directly ahead and she followed his gaze to where, at the far end of the green under the overhang of the trees, two girls sat on the bench by the churchyard wall. One was Jenny and the other was Dot.

'Twice in a morning.' Ralph laughed and twisted to speak over his shoulder. 'Joe, my boy, it could only happen on Midsummer Eve in the country.'

'Do shut up,' said Grace, 'or you'll give us both the creeps, won't he, Joe?'

'Joe won't say anything. Because he knows it's true.'

Two handsome, glamorous faces looked at him over the back of the seat and he felt like a rabbit trapped and bewitched by the bright and beautiful smiles of a brace of foxes. He shrugged and tried to speak but merely mumbled.

'Don't torment him,' said Grace.

'I wouldn't know how.'

'Oh yes you would.'

Ralph grinned, and twin sparks of great intensity seemed to be in his eyes.

'It's not I who torment you, is it, Joe? It's tall girls who run from you in the long grass.'

Grace was suddenly impatient. 'Oh, come on,' she said, 'we've got a lot to buy for this damned party of yours.'

'And that tall girl doesn't interest me a bit.' Joe

144

spoke vehemently. It was important that they should realize that he meant it. 'Diana means nothing to me.'

'But what do you mean to Diana?' Ralph was laughing at him as they got out of the car.

It was midday and the sun stood directly overhead, so bright it seemed almost to be audible, humming in the air. It had burned the sky behind the hills to the colour of copper, and Joe saw for the first time that the long thin triangle of grass was yellow and brown.

'How many will there be?' said Grace. 'We haven't even decided.'

'There are two over there for certain.' Ralph began to walk towards the girls, leaving Joe and Grace behind.

'I hope he knows what he is doing,' she said.

Joe walked beside her, keeping his eyes directly ahead. The churchyard wall was the colour of ash and the white light made the girls flimsy, like feathers of ash themselves.

'You don't want this party, do you?' he said.

'Not much.'

'But you don't want to be alone?'

'No.'

Joe, aware of his height alongside her, said foolishly, 'If you want to get away from them I'll protect you.'

She did not immediately answer, and they moved without speaking through grass that had been scythed ankle-high and now rattled brittle stems against their shoes. Joe clenched his jaw and bowed his head to watch his feet thrusting through the army of tiny spearmen; Gulliver in a hot country.

And then, at his side, she spoke.

'We'll see,' she said.

They walked slowly so that Ralph was in conversation with the girls before they arrived.

'One can't come,' he said. 'Dot has a date.'

'Ask him to come too,' said Grace.

'Can he?' He turned to Dot.

'Sorry, we've got to go somewhere.' Dot spoke quickly and it was a lie. She did not want to go to the big house.

'Pity.' Ralph took his attention away from her. 'Joe, it will have to be you with Grace.'

If he had meant to raise a smile he had failed but he did not appear to notice, or if he did notice he did not care. Jenny could see no faces because their heads were too close to the sun and she was still dazzled and squinting when Ralph said, 'But soft, who is this who treads the grass so daintily?'

'I might have known,' Dot murmured at Jenny's side.

Diana's skirts brushed the brittle stems as she came towards them.

'It's fate,' said Ralph to Joe. 'You'll have to accept it.' He held out an arm to welcome Diana to the group. 'You'd like to come to a party?'

'Oh yes, please!' Her hands, fingers interlocked and hidden, flew up to nestle under her chin.

'That's the sort of girl for us. Instant agreement; no questions asked.'

Diana fluttered her eyelids, taking on the part he had cast her in, and Dot stirred disgustedly on the bench.

'Midsummer Eve, Diana. We'll fetch you at nightfall.'

'How exciting!'

And then, because he remembered Joe's opinion of Diana, he said, 'Is there anybody you could bring? Male, I mean.'

'Well . . .' Diana's little lips were pressed into a

damp rosebud and her eyes slid sideways towards Joe.

Ralph laughed and punched Joe's arm. 'The long grass wins,' he said. 'Lie back and enjoy it.'

Joe felt the burning point of the sun between his shoulders. Diana would ruin everything. He was on the point of being utterly cruel with her when Grace, seeing what was in his mind, stepped forward.

'We'll look forward to seeing you, Diana,' she said. 'And now we must really get to the shop.' She passed between them, breaking up the group, and was about to lead the way across the grass when, suddenly, she hesitated and stopped.

'Oh no!' she said softly.

Mrs Goodchild stood at her cottage door, and at the sight of her Ralph laughed briefly and said, 'Shall we ask her, too?'

'I think she's rather sweet,' said Diana.

Ralph moved closer to Grace. 'You see,' he said, 'you are quite mistaken about the poor old thing.'

'I don't want to see her.'

Even as she spoke, the old woman began to move, stooping as she left her doorstep as though trying to find shelter in a storm of sunlight. Grace shrank back.

'Do you think she wants to speak to one of us?' said Diana, and at that moment Mrs Goodchild stood still and beckoned. 'Who?' Diana thrust her head forward, mouthing the question. 'Me?'

It was impossible to tell what the old woman's intention was, but Diana spoke to Grace. 'I don't think she wants me. It must be you.'

'I don't want to see her.' Grace backed away another step, but tried to cover her agitation. 'I've got a lot to do. She'd only hold me up.'

Diana became very sweet. 'I'll go to her if you like.'

Grace seized at the chance. 'Would you?' she said. 'Please.'

'Don't worry,' said Diana. 'You get on with your shopping. I'll see what she wants.'

They watched as she advanced on the small, bent figure, and saw her stoop, her hands between her knees, as one would bend towards a child to listen to what he said. After a moment, Diana straightened.

'It's all right,' she called, and waved for them to continue towards the shop. 'I'll see you tonight.'

She took the old woman's hand and began to walk with her back to the cottage.

'Huh,' said Dot, 'that's the first time I've seen her do that.'

But Diana, in front of all of them, was determined to be an Angel of Mercy. Before anyone had fully realized it she had gone with the old woman inside the cottage and closed the door behind them both.

'Well, that's one who isn't afraid of her,' said Ralph. He lingered beside the bench as Joe and his mother walked towards the store. 'I'd like to know what Diana and her find to say to each other.'

'Don't worry,' said Dot. 'You'll hear all about it.'

Ralph smiled at her and then spoke to Jenny. 'Something to look forward to tonight,' he said. 'Are you coming to help with the shopping?'

'No.' Jenny shook her head.

'All right.' He could see she was in no mood to talk. 'I'll pick you up later.'

Then the green was empty and Jenny sat without moving.

'You all right?' asked Dot.

Jenny nodded. But the way Grace had shrunk from the old woman had made something tighten within her. The noonday green was as still and as empty as

148

at midnight, and cold even though sparks of light glittered on fragments of stone, flared in the edges of windows, and made the motionless air appear to writhe as though the whole village, in torment, would burn itself away.

TWENTY-SIX

'Dot wants us all to be careful.' Jenny, holding the little rabbit in both hands, lifted it against the sky so that its back legs hung down, kicking wildly.

'You'll frighten it,' said Dot.

'We all have to be frightened now and again.' Jenny put her nose close to the little rabbit. 'Don't we?'

'I wish they'd never come here; not her nor her son.'

'Why not?' Jenny was crouching now, enclosing the rabbit in her lap.

'None of this would have happened. You'd still have been with Joe, and everything would have been all right.'

'Would it?' Jenny tilted her head sideways so that Dot looked down into her face.

For a moment, Dot hesitated and then, unable to stop herself, said with a kind of despair, 'Oh why are you so pretty, Jenny? It ain't fair.'

Jenny did not move or blush. Her grey eyes, very wide and childlike, regarded Dot calmly. 'Not everybody thinks so,' she said.

'He'll come back, Jenny. You don't have to worry.'

'Who will?'

'Joe, stupid.'

Jenny turned away. 'Who's he?'

'Well, he ain't Ralph!' Dot could not prevent her

true feelings coming out. 'You know Ralph ain't the one for you!'

'And Joe is?'

'See!' Dot's face was flushed. 'You didn't deny it.'

'You don't know anything about it.'

'Tell me to mind my own business.' Dot bit her lip.

'Ralph's the one I want. Isn't he, bunny? He's the one.'

'But Joe . . .' Dot could not keep the pain from her voice. 'It was always Joe.'

'He doesn't want me.' Jenny put her fingertip on the rabbit's nose. 'And I don't want him. We each have somebody else.'

'That damned Diana! What do he see in her?'

'Nothing much.' There was no emotion in Jenny's voice. 'I should have thought that was obvious.'

Dot's face was blank and she made no reply. Jenny stood up and handed her the rabbit.

'There you are, Dot,' she said, 'a present for you.'

Dot took the little creature and sat stroking it automatically as she pondered. 'Who is it then, Jen, if it ain't Diana?'

'Don't you know?'

Comically, so that Jenny smiled, Dot's eyes and mouth opened wide together. 'You don't mean . . .?'

Jenny nodded.

'That's awful, Jen!'

'I don't see anything awful in it. She's better looking than Diana.'

'Don't, Jen, you make me feel terrible.'

Once more Jenny spoke to the little rabbit. 'So now do you see why I hate him?'

'Don't go tonight, Jen.'

'I've got no choice.'

'Yes, you have.'

'Besides,' Jenny tickled the fur between the long, flattened ears, 'I want to.'

'You can't!'

'Don't worry, bunny.' Jenny straightened. 'I'll do what Auntie Dot says. I'll be careful.'

TWENTY-SEVEN

It was late, and gradually the lighted windows among the trees blinked and went out and the bottom of the village slid into a gentle darkness and slept.

Joe's father, though still reading in the high-backed chair by the empty grate, felt the heaviness of the day recede and he stirred as a moth, dancing around the lampshade in the middle of the ceiling, sent shadows over his newspaper. He was alone in the house, but he spoke aloud.

'All right,' he said, and laid the paper down. 'Time for bed.'

He rested his head on the back of the chair and lifted his eyes to where, like a woman's hand sewing, the moth looped and tapped at the shade. There was comfort in that and in the walls and the crowded furniture. She wasn't far away.

'Are the boys in bed?' said Jenny's father.

'Of course they are. Hours ago,' his wife replied.

'I thought I heard them lumping about up there.'

'Whether they're asleep is another matter. It's so hot.'

He went to close the window.

'What on earth are you doing that for?' she said.

'There's going to be a storm.'

'Storm, rubbish. The sky's clear. Look at the moon.'

'Can you smell those flowers?' he asked. There was

a flower bed against the wall under the window and the perfume penetrated the room. 'It's in their scent. Rain's coming.'

'Well, I hope it doesn't spoil Jenny's party.' She searched between the cushions and the edge of her chair, a nightly hunt for knitting needles.

'He seems a nice enough young chap, that Ralph,' said Mr Briggs.

Still searching, she said off-handedly, 'She won't marry him, if that's what you're thinking.'

'She's only a girl. And who said anything about marrying?'

'You did. It's what you meant, anyway.'

'Never. Not at all.' He closed the window. 'But now you've mentioned it,' he smiled, attempting to look sly. 'I wouldn't mind if she did.'

'Stupid.' Satisfied there were no needles, she stood up. 'It's still Joe, and always will be.'

'That's not my impression. Far from it.'

She ignored him. 'Who's going up first,' she said, 'you or me?'

'You go.'

She unlatched the door. 'You may know about storms,' she said. 'But you've got a long way to go before you understand your daughter.'

It was Ralph's idea that they should eat in the big dining room, spaced out around the large oval table on which stood two elaborate silver candlesticks, the only lighting he permitted. Apart from the chairs they sat on, there was no other furniture. Only his mother dared mention what Jenny knew they all must feel.

'No matter what you may think, Ralph, this room is too bare,' said Grace. 'I don't like it.'

She and Jenny sat at opposite ends of the long table, hidden from each other by the mound of light that the candles made between them. Jenny could only guess at the expression on her face but, whatever it was, Ralph had decided that mockery would be his answer.

He spoke to Jenny. 'My mother,' he said, 'has luxurious tastes.'

Jenny could think of nothing to say and let her eyes fall, gazing down into her plate. It had been like this all evening; the louder the conversation had grown with the wine the more silent she had become. And Joe also, further away from her on the other side of Diana, rarely spoke. It was only Diana who seemed to have entered into the spirit of the party as Ralph would have wished and it was to her, getting no answer from Jenny, that he now turned.

'What do you think of this room, Diana? Too sparse?'

She shook her head, let her hands flutter in the candlelight and laughed.

'You see.' He turned to the others. 'Diana and I, as true village people, prefer the simple life. You are all far too sophisticated for us.'

Once again Diana laughed, put her elbows on the table and made a white cup of her hands into which she placed her little chin. 'What I should really like,' she said seriously, 'would be to have this table in the middle of the field outside with just the candles burning.'

'And our feet in the long grass?'

'Particularly that.'

'Oh, Diana, how you fit into my dreams.'

Grace stood up to collect the plates and smiled at Jenny across the candles. 'Pay no attention to them,' she said, 'they've had too much to drink.'

'I don't mind,' said Jenny. It was an inept remark and she blushed, aware that Ralph deliberately did not look towards her. She had nothing to say to match his style and, as though physically he would wrench the party his way, he suddenly pushed himself back in his chair, both arms straight, the palms of his hands against the table edge.

'Of course this is the room where it all began.' There were deep lines in his cheeks but no hint of a smile in his voice.

Only Diana responded. 'Where what began?' she said.

'Where my mother met the rook and began to have fears of Mrs Goodchild.'

There was such a deliberate, if mysterious, cruelty in his voice that Diana's eyes flickered away from him and she said nothing. But he persisted.

'Isn't that so, Grace?' he said.

His mother stood where she was at the head of the table, very pale in the candlelight, and in the silence Joe got to his feet beside her and began to collect the plates.

'Oh, but I had forgotten,' said Ralph, and the sarcasm in his voice made Jenny's skin shrink with fear at the consequences of it, 'my mother has a protector. He removed the black and evil bird in his strong fist and would no doubt have removed Mrs Goodchild had he been asked.'

Joe tried to smile and Jenny's heart went out to him. His shyness and gentleness, both of which had seemed strangers to him since his mother's death, were visible again. He even put a finger to the bridge of his glasses.

But, as if to undermine it all, Diana spoke.

'I know what it must have been like,' she said, 'to be all alone and find that bird in here.' She shuddered elegantly. 'I know exactly how Grace felt.'

'Do you?' The sarcastic edge was in Ralph's voice as he turned to her, but none of them guessed it was because Diana had used his mother's name. He was beginning to tire of interlopers, all of them.

But Diana dared defy him. 'You wouldn't be so scornful,' she said, 'if you had heard what I was told this morning.'

'And what was that and where?'

'In Mrs Goodchild's house.'

In the cool room Jenny suddenly felt the heat of the sun that morning and saw the cottage door as it closed behind Diana. And something of the same was in Diana's mind for her eyes uncertainly sought his mother's permission to continue. Grace stood motionless and gave no sign.

'Tell me,' said Ralph.

Diana had become nervous. 'It's to do with the date,' she said and glanced again towards Grace, hoping for help.

'Date?' he asked.

She was reluctant, but she said, 'Midsummer Eve,' and closed her lips.

It was then that Grace drew in her breath, knowing that she had to speak, but she made them wait and looked at each one in turn as though accusing them all. And then she said, 'It was the night I promised to see Tom Goodchild on the hill. And didn't go.'

'Yes.' The tip of Diana's tongue appeared between the sipping lips, moistening them. She was nervous.

'So now you all know,' said Grace.

'I'm sorry,' said Diana. 'But she did want me to remind you.'

157

They faced each other, both rigid, both silent, until Ralph, full of impatience, broke in.

'Of what?' he said. 'Remind her of what?'

'It's all nonsense.' Diana tried hard to smile, but Ralph did not respond. He waited for an answer.

'All right.' Diana nodded, surrendering. 'She said her Tom would be there again. Tonight.'

Ralph had come forward, but now he thrust himself back from the table again and shouted with laughter.

'It's too good!' he said. 'Too good to miss. We must go to meet him.'

'No!' The cry came from Jenny, and even as it happened she knew she had to justify it before her shyness clamped down again. 'I've seen him!' The words came out in a rush. 'Your mother saw him, Joe!' His eyes were on her. 'We saw him just before she . . .'

Grace swayed slightly and stooped, placing her hands on the table to hold her weight. Joe moved as though to help her to a chair but she shook her head and murmured something.

'What?' Joe bent closer.

She raised her head and straightened. 'Don't worry about it, Joe. It was never anything to do with Betty. It was only me. I promised to meet him on the hill, not your mother.'

She pushed back her chair and walked out of the room. Even Ralph was silent, watching her go. Nothing, not even her departure, seemed to stir the air of the big room, and the candles burned with pure flames the shape of white drops.

'Tell us more, Jenny,' said Ralph.

She shook her head, looking at Joe, longing to tell him how she and his mother, as though brought together by Tom Goodchild, had known every important thing there was to know about each other before she died. For an instant their eyes met and held but then, deliberately, he turned, shattering whatever contact there was, and left the room.

Ralph did not appear to see him go. 'Diana,' he said, 'explain these village mysteries to me.'

And she was eager to do so, for only she and Ralph remained true to the spirit of the party. As she began to speak, Jenny stood up.

'You too?' he said, but made no attempt to rise.

Jenny nodded. She had to get out. She began to cross the room, moving from him, and he remained silent and did not move.

She closed the door behind her. Across the dark hall a strip of light showed where the kitchen door stood slightly open and there was the murmur of voices. She stood still for a moment trying to conquer the ache in her throat as she held back her tears, and then she crossed the hall and pushed at the door. She would call out goodnight and leave.

'Be kind to her, Joe.'

Grace stood at the far side of the kitchen, very tall and slim in her long black dress, but Joe, only a few feet from her, was taller.

'You've got to be kind, Joe.'

'Why?'

'Because she needs it. Ralph doesn't care. He's had too much to drink. He's simply deserted her.'

'So you've decided I must take over.'

'That expression on your face, Joe. It does not improve your looks.'

'I'm going to stay with you,' he said. 'That's what we intended.'

She shook her head and he saw the thin silver chain at her throat move like a drop of water against

159

her skin. She lowered her eyes and he took a step nearer.

'I'm going to stay with you.'

With her head bowed she was very young and she did not move as he reached for her. His hand brushed her bare shoulder.

'You promised,' he said softly.

At that moment, when it was cruellest, she threw back her head and looked at him directly. Her eyes were not those of a girl.

'What are you trying to say, Joe?' She was her full age. She needed nothing else to protect her. It was Joe who moved back half a step.

'You promised,' he repeated, but he was a boy, pleading.

'I promised nothing.'

She lifted her eyes from him and suddenly she stiffened, gazing beyond his shoulder. He saw that something had held her attention, but he was reluctant to turn away from her. He began to speak, but a tiny movement of her hands stopped him. He turned slowly.

Jenny stood in the doorway, the light full on her. She had seen every stage of his humiliation.

Silence and darkness pressed in to deafen and blind him. For a full second she watched, and then was gone.

A door was wrenched open. Feet scuffled the gravel outside. Before either of them had moved she was out of the house and running to where the road curved down into the hidden village.

TWENTY-EIGHT

Grace saw his face change.

'Joe.'

She put out a hand towards him but could not touch him. The torrent of his sensations had jolted to a halt and frozen to make a skin outside his skin.

'Where are you going?'

He did not once look back and she ran after him out of the kitchen, but he was gone. The hall door was open and she ran out into the field. The air was cold, spilling down over the hills as the clouds pushed in to fill the sky. Jenny was still on the drive, almost out of sight, but Joe was not following her.

Wildly, Grace turned, gathering up the hem of her dress, attempting to walk into the long grass as she stared towards the bare hilltop, but the heels of her shoes twisted and she stumbled. There was no sign of him anywhere and she ran back into the house for Ralph.

'Jenny!'

Ralph's voice was faint and far away and she could not see him against the darkness of the house.

'Jenny!'

A shift in the air pressed a deep ripple in the grass and she watched it sweep like a long arm around the house and fade in the distance. It had failed to gather her. She began to cry, letting the tears run down her face, waiting to hear him call her once more but knowing that she would not return.

'Jenny!'

She backed into the path between the tall hedges and stopped, listening again. The candles glimmered within the room, but they were as pale as milk and the window was blank and sightless. She thought she heard the sound of footsteps far away on the gravel near the house and guessed that he had gone round the corner, leaving her.

And then she heard him again but his voice was very faint now with the house between, and he was no longer calling her. It was Joe's name she heard, and when it came again she turned and ran.

The gap in the hedge was narrow, but Joe thrust into it so that the thorns would drag at the shame that enveloped him. He leant against them and let his shirt tear. But it was only cloth.

He heard his name. She wanted him back at the house. She wanted to see him return.

When the call came again he put his back to the thorns and pressed until he felt them burn through his skin into his blood.

Jenny had no coat and her dress was thin but it was not until she emerged from the long tunnel of trees that she felt that the air had turned chill. She ignored it and wandered slowly over the green to the bench by the churchyard wall. The tears had dried on her face but her eyes were still moist. She made no attempt to dry them.

That his skin had opened was no comfort to him. Such a small pain could not reach deep enough to overthrow the anguish that drove him higher up the hill. And over the crest of it a cool breeze flooded down as though to soothe and, at the same time, mock him.

Automatically, Jenny's fingertips sought along the bench for a paint bubble to prick, but all she found were the ragged edges of empty craters. She sat where she was and let the night absorb her. Beyond the bridge and the piled up blackness of the trees the moon had begun a sullen battle with the clouds, and at her feet the long triangle of grass tilted or sank as the light swelled or faded.

In the house they had moved to a room where Grace could stand at the window with the hill in full view. One small lamp in the corner gave a subdued light, and in the shadows Ralph sat in one of the low chairs and Diana had curled her legs beneath her to sit on the floor so that he could bend over her. They murmured together.

Grace clenched her fists. 'Why has he gone up there?' she said. 'What is he doing?'

They were slow to turn their heads towards her and when they did so their eyes were unfocused. They had not heard her and they did not care. Soon they turned away, oblivious of her.

He was still in the shadow of the hillside when he saw Tom Goodchild's hanging place. Three trees stood on the bare hilltop, their arms thrown out to embrace the clouds that rushed towards them.

When they mingled, he began to climb again, his mind made up.

Jenny got to her feet and began to walk alongside

the churchyard wall to the narrow road where Joe's cottage stood. The house was lightless but she stood outside it and thought of his mother, the one person to whom she could have talked. But she was gone, sleeping close to the church. Jenny crossed the road to where the little gate let into the graveyard. Beyond this point, it was all at an end.

Behind her, in the cottage garden, the air shifted like the deep currents of the sea and the scent of the flowers lifted on a slow wave and pushed into the bedroom. Joe's father stirred, frowned slightly, and then, like a swimmer, turned on his back and floated, fast asleep on the barely perceptible rise and fall of a calm ocean.

Level with Joe, the moon, like a white furnace mouth, writhed with smoke and then went out. He stood in the darkness of the hill and heard the first rain whisper along the ridge towards him.

Beyond this point the sleepers lay, but Jenny was unafraid. The gate swung to behind her, shutting as softly as a bedroom door, and she began to walk up the churchyard slope.

His mother's grave lay at the foot of the church where the path branched to run towards the rectory on one side and the tall iron gates on the other. It was unmarked as yet, except by the flowers. Jenny crouched to tidy them as the first drops of rain tapped on the leaves and into the grass around her.

Joe knew Tom Goodchild's pain, the exact shape of his limbs where he stood and reached to the branches. He put himself there and let the rain enclose him coldly.

The foot of the tall iron gate scraped the ground and

Jenny raised her head. The shadows under the trees were deep and she could see nothing, but she knew Mrs Goodchild was there. She stood up, beyond any feeling of fear now and even wanting to talk with the old woman, but as she rose her glance swept the slope. And stopped.

Joe took off his shirt and began to twist it in his hands.

Taller than the gravestones, a figure stood below her on the slope.
'Ralph?'
She knew her voice was too soft to reach him.
'Ralph?'
He had followed her from the house.
'Ralph!'
She shouted this time and pulled back, and as she did so the smell of the flowers swirled with her, sweet and corrupt.
She shrieked at him, forcing anger over fear, making her voice lunge at him.
'Is that you?'
But she knew.

Joe twisted the shirt in his fists, tighter, pulling it into a rope.

Jenny saw a narrow head with short hair. His ears were large and his mouth, too big for his hollow cheeks, was slightly open. His clothes did not fit well. His eyes were closed.
Backwards now, on the path, towards the shut church. Backwards.
Tap, tap on her shoulder.

She twisted. It was rain. The old woman, hidden in shadow, still blocked the gate.

The moon went and she could see nothing on the path. Her breath caught like a solid thing in her throat and she froze, listening.

The wind lifted out of the graveyard and moaned in the road like a coward. Only the rain remained, filling the slope with one long whisper, touching her hands and arms with threads and beginning a thin little laugh in the gutters of the church as the moon came again, briefly.

He was on the path. Tom Goodchild. Coming towards her. Stepping slowly on clumsy feet.

She ran for the rectory. In the tunnel of the hedge she thrashed her arms at whatever might be there and beat her way through the copse on the other side and out onto the safety of the lawn.

And he was there. He stood on the lawn between her and the rectory. Head bowed. In the rain.

She turned. The copse had closed behind her.

And then he began to move, coming towards her, dragging his feet. She spun and her wet hair caught across her mouth. She whimpered and backed away, all hope gone, along the edge of the trees, further from the dark rectory, leaving it behind, further and further away, driven along the lawn's edge to where shrubs held it in.

She sank against them, falling through wet leaves that slid like deep water around her until she crawled on a shelving bank and was out on the bare hillside, up and running towards his hanging place.

Joe reached to a branch.

The rain, in shafts and columns, ran with her up

the slope. She looked back, and he was still there, limping upwards, his head dipping and rising like a boat's prow in heavy seas.

The wet rope caught in a fork and he ran his hand down it.

She saw him reach, stretched between branch and ground, elongated. Tom Goodchild had leapt ahead and was repeating his death. She screamed.

He turned in the shriek of the wind and saw her.

She retreated. A tree touched her shoulder and her head fell back, her mouth open, under water, drowning.

He caught her as she slid to the ground. Marble. Cold as marble. Both of them. He lifted her and her eyes flickered, seeing the rain run in extra sinews on his arm, and she was without weight for him.

A voice from somewhere far below lifted towards them, as thin as a bird's cry, calling his name.

She stiffened in his arms. 'What's that!'

'They are looking for us.'

He walked down from the ridge with her into the shelter of the slope and put her down. The cry came again and then once more but fainter.

'They are giving up,' he said.

She twisted, looking back to where the trees still lashed.

'I saw him!' she said. 'Tom Goodchild made me go up there.'

The rain, gentler down here, brushed the turf.

'You smell of the rain, Jenny.'

His lips touched hers and the rain ran from his face to hers.

'You taste of the grass,' he said.

'I am green and cold. Perhaps I am dead.'

167

'Both of us,' he said. 'Both of us dead.'

They lay on the grass under the rain, but suddenly she thrust her hands into the wet hair of his head and pulled him towards her savagely.

'We were,' she said. 'We were dead.'

Through the coldness of the rain and the coldness of their skin heat ran like liquid. Joe heard himself saying words that he had never heard before.

'There is no death that dying doth not overcome.'

TWENTY-NINE

'Must we start so early, Grace?' Ralph raised his head to see her standing in his bedroom door.

'I want to go.' She touched her forehead with her fingertips and closed her eyes. 'I must see your father.'

'He'll be here in a couple of days.'

'I must see him.' She turned away. 'But I can go alone.'

'Not in your present state.' He pushed back the covers and sat up in his camp bed. 'Your shoes,' he said, 'they're wet.'

'I've been out.'

'Where?'

'Walking.'

'It's a bright morning.' He yawned to cover what they both knew was a question. 'There should be a good view from the top of the hill.'

'Yes,' she said. 'It is a lovely day.'

So the hill was bare and no disaster had overcome Joe.

He swung his legs over the edge of the bed and stood up, barefoot on the bare floorboards. He wore no pyjama jacket and his arms were as thin as sticks as he raised them above his head to yawn again. 'So the storm is over.'

'Yes.'

'Are we coming back tonight?'

'You may if you wish.'

'But you are not?' His thin face was serious. She thought he looked very young; much younger than when he smiled.

'No,' she said.

'And tomorrow?'

'I don't know.'

'Ah well.' He went to the foot of his bed to pick up his clothes. 'I shall not be sorry to sleep in a decent bed again.'

The sun reached through the window and touched her as she lay naked under the single sheet. It was early and the linen was as cool as rain except for the hot touch of the sun. Jenny slid her legs and thought of Joe.

She sat up. One thing remained.

The house was still asleep, unprivileged, as she crept downstairs. Outside, flowers bowed their heads as though the wind still pressed on them but they were bright, and as she stooped to pick a bunch of marigolds quick drops of rain fell from them. Quietly she walked out into the road and looked up at the windows. The curtains were all closed and nobody saw her as she walked towards the village.

The sunlight had reached the row of cottages as she crossed the green but the woodwork of the door, when she tapped on it, was still cold and the rain-scoured step was only patchily dry. It was a long minute before the old woman stood there, blinking.

'Some flowers.' Jenny held out the marigolds. 'For Tom.'

The old jaws chewed before an answer came, and then she said, 'He were a good boy.'

'Yes,' said Jenny.

'He never did no one no harm. He only ever wanted for people to like him.' She took the flowers in a skinny hand and the almost opaque eyes looked up from them to Jenny. 'Nobody have ever brung him anything before.'

'I know,' said Jenny.

The narrow head with the thin hair nodded.

'Mrs Goodchild.' Jenny put a hand on the old woman's thin fingers. 'Tom can rest now.' She knew it was true. Through Joe and herself he had obliterated his own anguish. By saving them he had freed himself of his own misery.

Mrs Goodchild was still nodding. 'He always were a lovely old boy, my Tom.'

A car came almost silently from the road behind the cottages, nosed its way on to the bridge and flashed and winked there momentarily in the morning sun before it tilted and slid away down the further side, turning to run alongside the swollen river down the valley. Neither of them saw it.

ABOUT THE AUTHOR

The Ghost on the Hill is John Gordon's first novel for
The Viking Press. About writing for young people he
says, "it is always an attempt to get to the edge of things,
to reach that strangest of all places where one thing ends
and another begins. . . . Within a story there must be a
reality that is all but touchable, a place in which things
can happen. The starting point must be a place that
already exists. . . . The boundary between imagination
and reality, and the boundary between being a child
and being an adult are border country, a passionate
place in which to work."

Mr. Gordon is married and has two children. He lives
in Norwich, England.